STRANGER AT MY TABLE

Letters From the Past Series

TINA CLOUGH

STRANGER AT MY TABLE

Copyright © Tina Clough 2023

The author asserts her moral right to be identified as the author of this work.

PAPERBACK ISBN 978-1-99-118713-0

Lightpool Publishing

www.lightpoolpublishing.com

Cover and book design by Andrene Low

Part I

Miranda drove down the M5 on auto pilot, deep in thought. What would it be like, she wondered, this first time after the funeral, with a whole week to catch up with friends and meet with Gramma's lawyer. It was hard to believe that she had been back from New Zealand for a year already and in all those trips back to Exeter, she never stayed more than a night or two. Enough time to visit her grandmother in the hospital, to sit beside her bed and hold her unresponsive hand for a few hours while talking to her, telling her about her job and her friends. She refused to believe that Gramma couldn't hear what she said after that awful head injury, as one of the nurses had told her. The only possible way to cope with it had been to believe that somewhere inside her head Gramma listened, and felt her hand being held, was comforted. Miranda knew had been in a strange place mentally on her trips back to Exeter, unable to socialize or enjoy anything in the vicinity of her poor grandmother lying there like an effigy in that silent room, so much so that she never spent more than an hour having coffee or lunch with any of her old friends.

Maybe she would be back to her normal Exeter persona this time, maybe burying Gramma had put a full stop to that awful time and she would feel like socializing again and having some fun. She smiled to herself, glad she had taken the plunge and made a decision to ask for a week off.

On an impulse, she turned off the M5 at Taunton, and that little decision was proof that this trip was different, that this time she would have the time to do things simply because she wanted to. She had always liked the Blackdown Hills and the different landscape along this road coming in to Exeter from a different, slower angle, not just geographically, but with a different feel to it, too.

She arrived just in time to book into the Mercure Exeter Hotel and put her suitcase in her room before it was time to go to the meeting with Donna. The receptionist recognized her from a month ago, when she came for her grandmother's funeral and smiled. 'Welcome back! I see you're here for a bit longer this time.'

'Yes, a week - enough time to see all my old friends and make it a bit of a holiday.'

She knew that her friends would protest when they discovered that she was staying here again rather than at Thornhill or with one of them, but she had enjoyed it here when she came for the funeral. Not staying alone at Thornhill, moving around that vast empty house where she had never spent more than a few nights on her own. Being right in town seemed a better option this time and she hadn't had a holiday or paid for anything much for a year. There would be plenty of time to get Thornhill tidied up and fit for her to stay another time: she needed time to get used to the idea of staying at Thornhill without Gramma there. It doesn't seem like my childhood home now, she thought, well, yes it does, but it's very strange.

Walking to Donna's office on this sunny April day it felt as if she had nearly forgotten what a pretty town Exeter was. It was as if she were looking at it with an outsider's eyes and seeing it for the first time. And lovely spring weather helped, a complete change from those two rainy days a month ago, when nothing felt right, and the grey veil of sadness lay over everything. Today the cathedral glistened nearly white in the sun and a tour bus was disgorging its passengers. She skirted a cluster of seniors taking photos and looked up at the intricately carved medieval façade. The day was warmer than she had anticipated, so she peeled off her jacket as she walked and glanced at her watch; ten past three. Her appointment was at quarter past, so she increased her pace and made it with one minute to spare.

Sitting in Donna Irwin's waiting room Miranda studied the photographs of serious men framed in black, some in court garb of gowns and wigs, some in old fashioned suits and high shirt collars holding themselves ramrod straight. There were two older Irwin's in the line-up of former partners in the firm and she recognized Donna's father, who has now retired. He came to Thornhill after her grandfather's funeral when she was eighteen and embarrassed her by studying her face in silence for what seemed an inordinately long moment when they shook hands. She can still recall the uncomfortable feeling of being under scrutiny in a way she had not experienced before, and her grandmother putting a hand on her shoulder as if to protect her.

'Well, then!' said Donna decisively when they were seated in her office, which looked as if nothing had changed since the early days of the last century. 'Sorry I'm late, but some of my older clients take their time, particularly when I visit them in their homes – it can be hard to get away without being rude, they love to talk. When I saw you after the funeral you had so many people wanting to see you and then you had to go back to Bristol nearly directly, so we never had a formal meeting. But you knew all about the will already, of course - I told you the details when you returned after Mrs. Carlow's accident.'

'It was such a scramble,' said Miranda apologetically. 'I'm sorry I had to say I couldn't possibly see you after the funeral, but we are working on the plans for a big project and we were at a tricky stage just then, so I had no choice but go back straight away.'

'No matter – all we need to do today is tidy up the final details, now the probate has been processed. There was nobody who could contest your right to inherit your grandmother's entire estate. Your only living relatives are third cousins who have no claim, of course, so it was a simple process and Thornhill is now yours. I have applied for the title deed to be changed to your name and you should get a notification by email any day now. And the same with the invested money, which is in Government bonds, your grandmother left it that way after her husband's death. The bonds have also been transferred to your name. I'll send you a link to the DMO in case you decide to move the money elsewhere.'

'What's the DMO?'

'It's the government's portal for debt management – your asset is their debt, you understand. You'll be able to manage things from there yourself very easily and if you don't want to be bothered with it, you can consult an investment broker or ask us to do it. There's quite a tidy sum left, even after your grandmother's lengthy hospital costs, which were considerable. As you know, we cashed in some of the bonds to pay for her care. The expenses for the house this last year were paid out of the bond interest that comes into our trust account.'

Miranda realised she had never thought very much about this and shook her head at her own lack of care. 'You know, I think I was so upset and traumatized after I rushed home from New Zealand, what with my grandmother so horribly injured and all the worry, that I never really paid much attention to it. I knew she had given me power of attorney, but I just told you to take care of it and you've been doing it ever since. Thank you!'

Donna's plain middle-aged face crinkled in a smile. 'It's what we do – we take care of all those things. And we've been paid from the money in the trust account - as per my emails to you once a quarter. But I want to tell you how things stand right now, so you're up to date and can just carry on. It seems a bit strange that the house has sat empty for nearly a year, but I don't suppose either of us expected her to linger so long with such a head injury and in a coma. The council tax has been paid and the diesel tank for the central heating was topped up at the end of March, so it's ready for the colder weather in October - which we don't seem to get until November these days.' She made a face. 'The only advantage of climate change, I suppose. But anyway, the annual insurance premium for the property and the contents will fall due again in August. Since you returned from New Zealand I haven't been out there, but you said you would visit occasionally, so I presume everything is all right?'

'Oh, yes – I've come down every now and then since the accident, just for the day to visit my grandmother. I always went out to Thornhill and walked around and checked nobody had broken any windows or broken in. Last time I didn't go in, but I picked daffodils in the garden, they were all out. That man you hired to mow the lawns had just been and it looked nearly like it used to expect for the weeds in the flower beds. I suppose he might as well continue for the time being and just send his invoices to me instead of to you?'

'Of course - and you have no thoughts of living there yourself, getting a job nearby? Thornhill is such a gorgeous place.'

Miranda shook her head again and smiled at the idea. 'I can't see myself rattling around in that huge place – six bedrooms! There used to be seven, but my grandparents used one of them to create two extra bathrooms when I was little. I don't know what my great-great-grandfather was thinking when he built it – they only had three children. But I suppose it was a status thing back then, a self-made man from a humble background who became really wealthy and wanted the world to know it.'

And then it struck her that she still didn't know how much money there was. 'How much *is* invested? I don't think I ever asked, and I'd love to buy a new car even before I sell the house, if there's enough for that. The one I bought when I came back from New Zealand is nearly twenty years old, but I had very little money just then, having bought the air ticket and whatever.'

'Good heavens – you should have told me,' said Donna. 'I could have passed the insurance money for your grandmother's car straight to you instead of having it sitting in the trust account.'

She put her hand on the yellow folder on her desk and looked as if she felt like laughing. 'Four hundred and ninety thousand pounds in total between what's in our trust account and the invested money, so you'll definitely be able to afford a new car. We'll forward the amount left in our trust account, less our final costs, directly to your bank. And, of course, a complete account of all the transactions. All the other paperwork is in the folder, insurance papers and the last invoices we paid, so you know exactly who's been paid and for what - and the letter left by your grandfather to be handed to you when your grandmother died, or when you turned thirty, whichever occurred first.'

Miranda stared at her, confused. For a moment she forgot to even be surprised at the amount of money her grandmother left, a totally unexpected amount that she hadn't expected after a year of expensive hospital care.

'What do you mean? A letter from my grandfather? He died ten years ago. And why the strange conditions?'

'I don't know. The sealed envelope was left here when you were fifteen or sixteen, at the time your grandfather first knew he had cancer, and it's been in the family's deed box in our strong room ever since. I imagine whatever is in it will be something he wanted you to know, but perhaps your grandmother didn't agree. It sounds like something from the Victorian era, doesn't it? But it happens now and then.'

Miranda got a feeling that Donna had a theory she was holding back, so she reached out for the folder and Donna pushed it across the desk without comment.

'If you want to open it now, I'll leave you alone for a few minutes — I don't know what it is, but it could be … emotional perhaps?'

She thinks she knows, and it's something that is going to upset me, or maybe her father told her, thinks

Miranda, perhaps he knew what Granda wrote and then he told Donna.

'Yes, perhaps I had better read it alone,' she said, and Donna left the room and closed the door behind her.

Chapter 2

Miranda opened the folder and right at the front, not attached to the clip holding loose papers together, was an envelope with her full name on the front: Miranda Caroline Carlow. She recognized his handwriting though she hadn't seen it for over ten years, and on the back the conditions Donna had mentioned:

To be opened on the death of my wife Margaret or on Miranda's 30th birthday, whichever comes first.

She worked her forefinger under the flap and ripped the envelope open; inside was a single sheet of plain paper, printed with only the last line in handwriting.

Darling Miranda

I know this will be upsetting for you, but you have a right to know, and when I and Gramma are gone there will be nobody left to tell you.

You have always known that your mother died aged 20, just before you turned two, either from an accidental drug overdose (as in the coroner's findings) or by suicide. We will never know, but I find it hard to believe she took her own life when she had you to look after — she adored you. You also know that on your birth certificate there is no father's name.

Your father was my uncle (on my mother's side) - Jimmie Croft (James). He worked in the music industry, managed artists and dabbled in TV productions. He stayed here once for a week and started what would these days be called 'grooming' our darling Jess, and shortly after this she ran away to live with him in London. He was 68 and she had just turned 17. When she became pregnant, he took up with someone else and instead of coming back to live with us, Jess lived in rather dreadful circumstances. It took us a long time to find out exactly where she was and by that time you had been born. She refused our help and said she had got herself into a mess and would take responsibility.

We paid for her to come for visits, and she did come quite frequently, bringing you with her, but after a year we started getting worried. Her appearance was changing, at times both she and you were dirty, she got very thin, and she stole cash from us, though we always gave her money when she went back to London and also offered to give her a regular allowance. She refused to tell us where she lived, and it was only after her death that we found out that she had been working in the sex industry sharing a flat with three other girls (sex workers).

We brought you up from then on and you have been such a joy to us both, clever and kind and cheerful. I know I'm going to die from this cancer in the not too distant future, and I doubt that Margaret will tell you the background, so here it is — and remember it doesn't change who you are or what you are!

Your ever loving, Granda

She sat perfectly still and tried to take it in, then she read the letter again, folded it slowly and put it back in the envelope. They say everyone has a secret, she thought, and my grandparents certainly did. She searched her memory for earlier clues, anything that could have alerted her, then the door opened and Donna returned. She walked around the desk and sat down, looking carefully at Miranda, who returned the look without comment.

'Well, then. I can see you've read the letter - and I think I know what was in it.'

Miranda handed her the envelope. 'You might as well read it and then you can tell me if it is what you thought it would be.'

Donna pulled out the sheet of paper, read rapidly and just like Miranda, her eyes went back to the top and she read it again.

'Ah — I never knew for sure who it was,' she said. 'My father told me a little, not exactly who it was, but I knew Mrs. Carlow regarded it as incest. Legally it's not - as your father and his uncle did not have what's called a lineal relationship, which is just a phrase meaning in a direct descending line.'

'But my grandmother thought it was incest - and perhaps my grandfather did too,' said Miranda. 'And she wanted to hide it from me, and he wanted me to know, but he didn't want to do something that would upset her. You're right – it's a bit like a Victorian novel, isn't it? I can't remember ever meeting that ... whatever he would be to me, great uncle and father rolled into one or something like it? I don't think I've ever heard his name mentioned before today – I suppose they barred the doors and never saw him again?'

'You're probably right. And *are* you upset?' Donna tilted her head and looked carefully at her. 'You always look so composed that I can't tell – you get that from Mr. Carlow, I think. If you need it, you might consider counselling, perhaps? But I must say you don't look as if you're in shock.'

'Oh no! I'm not *that* upset,' said Miranda, and thought maybe she ought to be. She was surprised, that was all. 'I know these things happen, but I *am* surprised. I can't remember anything about spending the first two years of my life in a flat full of sex workers, and I have no memory of my mother at all, or of being neglected, nothing! Perhaps at that age you don't remember things. You think you do, but it's just what people have told you afterwards and photos you've seen. I feel very sad that my mother died so young and in such circumstances - that's a tragedy in the real sense of the word. And I am seriously upset about that Jimmie person, I refuse to call him my father. Fancy doing whatever it was he did, pushed her out, abandoned her or something, and not taking responsibility, not making sure she was all right. What a bastard!'

'Oh, absolutely − I agree totally, 'said Donna warmly. 'He used her, and when she got pregnant, she was a hindrance, and he discarded her. And perhaps he wanted her to have an abortion and she refused, who knows? What did you think your mother had died of, before today, I mean?'

'I knew she died of drug taking − my grandfather told me when I was about twelve or so. He said she got into bad company and ran away from home. And it *is* what happened, isn't it? He just left out a couple of facts.'

They sat silent for a minute, and Miranda thought of what she had remembered when she sat in the waiting room, when she looked at the photos on the wall. How Donna's father came to the house after her grandfather died, and how he looked so disconcertingly at her.

Now she got to her feet and picked up her bag. 'I've got to go, Donna, I'm meeting an old school friend for dinner, and I have some errands to do first. Thank you for everything you've done, we'll obviously stay in touch.'

'When are you going back?'

'I've taken a week off. I thought I'd start going through things at Thornhill, and then

go back on Sunday.'

Telling Donna that she had errands to do was partly true and partly an excuse. She could perform her errand any day this week, but she suddenly felt a need to get away from that brown-panelled room, the discussion about her mother and the nearly Dickensian atmosphere it engendered.

A strong room full of deed boxes! The thought made her smile as she walked out into the bright sunshine, and she wondered if all lawyers still talked about deed boxes and strongrooms. Or was it just in this particular firm where time seemed to have stopped? It seemed so quaint, but the law profession was quaint in a nearly theatrical way. Those horrible wigs, she thought with a shudder, but I suppose they add gravitas.

The first second-hand shop she went to was disappointing, basically too orderly and tidy for the sort of massed treasure she was hoping for, and it only took a quick circuit to make sure there was nothing there for her. The second place looked more promising even from outside, the window crammed full of diverse objects that bore no relation to each other and no attempt had been made to create a deliberate display. This is my sort of shop, thought Miranda and went in, it's a potential treasure trove. The middle-aged man behind the counter called out a greeting and offered assistance, but she said that she was only looking, so he went back to his newspaper. Walking slowly around the shop that turned out to include two smaller rooms at the back, she let her gaze sweep over every horizontal surface. She scanned the objects displayed on chests of drawers and sideboards, in bookcases and glass-fronted cabinets and picked a thing up here and there. When she put four small ceramic bowls on the counter the assistant said, 'I see you like pottery,' and got sheets of newspaper out from under the counter, but Miranda smiled. 'Yes, but I haven't finished yet - I was just off-loading.'

Returning to the exact point where she left off, she continued until she had made four trips back to the counter and the possibilities had been exhausted. The collection of bowls and dishes on the counter had the assistant puzzled.

'You must excuse me, but I'm really curious now. Nine small bowls and dishes, two medium sized bowls - some are pottery and some are china, and nearly all are dark colours. But none of them match, so you're not collecting a set, it's very intriguing. Please tell me what you are going to do with them - if you don't mind?'

Miranda looked at the line-up on the counter with

great satisfaction and said with a straight face. 'I'm going to break them.' She had used this throw-away line many times before and she always enjoyed the look on people's faces when she said it, and today's shop assistant was no exception. 'You're going to break them!? Why?'

She got her phone out and opened the photo gallery, selected one image and held the phone up. 'I make these.'

He took the phone and looked closely at the image of a small dark grey bowl veined with gold and handed the phone back. 'Very beautiful! I've heard of this, a Japanese method for mending things, isn't it?'

'Kintsugi,' said Miranda and slid the phone back in her pocket. 'It's an ancient technique for mending broken objects by mixing gold or silver powder with the glue and making the joins a feature.'

'And then you sell them?'

'Yes, I sell them as art objects via a gallery in Bristol.' She fished in her bag. 'They're very popular, and sometimes people bring in something precious thye've broken and the gallery commissions me to mend it using this technique.'

'Is it difficult to do?'

'It's time consuming and you need a lot of patience. You can only glue one shard at a time and then let the glue dry before you continue. The hardest thing is learning how to break them, so they come apart in three or four pieces without too much chip damage to the glaze.'

He seemed more than usually interested and she wondered if he was thinking of doing this himself, but he surprised her.

'If you like, I can put things aside for you, now that I know exactly what you're looking for,' he said. 'I get a lot of stuff donated. You know, when people clear out their parents' houses. And sometimes I go to auctions and buy boxes of assorted things. At the moment a lot of people who were young and newly married in the sixties and seventies are going into rest homes or moving to smaller houses – or dying. We're getting more and more stuff with this kind of look now. Ten years ago, we hardly had any – it's a generation change. And by the way, my name's Clive.'

Miranda paid and gave him her card and he looked surprised. 'So, you're not a fulltime artist then? I see you're an engineer. Is this more like a hobby?'

'It's a sideline, I suppose you could say, but my real job is in engineering. I could never support myself doing kintsugi full-time. It's too slow and I'd either need to work sixteen hours a day every day of the week or charge so much that they didn't sell.' She smiled at his thoughtful expression. 'But keep the card, and if you hear of someone who has broken something precious or cracked it badly, you can give them my contact details. I like doing the repair work – it's interesting because people tell me the background of the piece, often it's family history. But I don't get to do it very often, three or four times a year at most.'

'I'll keep your card in the till,' he said and started wrapping the bowls in newspaper, then suddenly he chuckled. 'I was going to say, I'll wrap them properly, so they don't break, but if one of them does, it doesn't matter, does it? It might break in just the right way.'

Within a couple of minutes of leaving the shop she regretted leaving her old Volvo at the hotel. The box was impossible to carry under her arm, so she put it down, slipped her jacket back on, and piled her bag and the folder on top of the bowls in the box. Holding the box with both hands she continued through Cathedral Close and down along the trees, grateful for the shade, but by the time she was back at the hotel her arms were aching and she was seriously overheated.

Chapter 3

Amber arrived ten minutes late after sending a text to say she had been delayed, and Miranda smiled at her hurried entrance into the bar. 'You look just like I did about a couple of hours ago! Hot and rushed.'

They embraced and remained standing beside the table, looking fondly at each other. 'God, you look great!' Amber and ran a hand over her own dark bob, in a habitual gesture that made Miranda smile. 'I don't know how you always turn up looking about eighteen, however long you've been away. Are you on some youth drug or something? I'm beginning to look just like my mum – and I'm not quite thirty. Tilly took a photo of me the other day when we were having drinks, and I couldn't believe how much I look like Mum these days.'

Miranda said what she always said when someone commented on how young she looked. 'I take after my grandmother, you know that. It's the Viking genes from a thousand years ago or whatever it was. After the Romans left anyway. Remember how she barely looked fifty when she was sixty-five and we were about to leave school, and I discovered some of our friends had always thought she was my mother. And your mum is gorgeous!'

After an hour at their little round table, they ordered tapas instead of going into the restaurant to have a proper meal.

'I like this room – it's kind of old-looking though it's quite new, very comfortable' says Amber. 'Tilly and I came here a few weeks ago, so I could meet her boyfriend. That's when she took that photo of me.'

'What? Your lesbian sister has a boyfriend now? That's a surprise, she always seemed so staunchly gay.'

'Don't ask me! Maybe she's bi-sexual. She's really keen on this guy, besotted actually! And here's to whatever happens next!' Amber raised her glass in a toast. 'His name is Harold, and he seems nice, very tidy and conventional looking, tall - nice body. And he comes out with the funniest things. Here we were, surrounded by other people, it was quite busy, it was a Friday night, and he said, "I like having sex with a lifelong lesbian, less chance of HIV and some other nasties". He didn't lower his voice or anything, and the older couple beside us just about choked on their drinks. I don't quite know what to make of him, not quite my cup of tea I don't think, but so long as Tilly's happy, I'm not going to complain.'

Miranda grinned. 'Of course, you'll complain – you'll be forever telling me his bad points, if it turns out he has any. You know you're famous for never leaving an annoying topic alone. And how is Torsten? Why is he away for so long?'

'He's gone back to Denmark for a while – his dad needed him to come back and run the business for a few weeks. He had surgery on a ruined shoulder and got a whole new joint, and now he's not allowed to lift anything for a while and he can't work on a computer, so Torsten went back. His brother's in the army and he's away somewhere in Africa now with the UN, and somcone's got to help produce all that lovely Danish butter.'

By the time they had caught up on gossip about school friends and teachers it was getting late, and Miranda had just smothered a yawn when Amber suddenly remembered why Miranda had come. 'How did it go at the lawyer's – was it about the house?'

Lightning-fast Miranda had to decide how much to tell her. On the one hand they were best friends and had known each other since their first year at school, and on the other hand she needed to think through everything she had learnt today and what the implications were. It was probably best to avoid talking about money for the time being, or her parentage. People must have known that her grandparents had money, but the surprising amount, which she had not yet had time to adjust to herself, was nobody else's business.

'Yes, all about title deeds and council tax and central heating bills and whatever – lots of detail that I need to know, if I'm selling the house.'

'If?' Amber stared at Miranda. 'Is it an "if"? Do you mean you might keep it?'

It must have been my subconscious that made me say that, thought Miranda. 'No, not really – I don't know why I said that. It's such a monster of a house and what on earth would I do with it? It's not as if I'm married with six kids or about to take in foster children. I'll probably sell it in the middle of the summer when the garden looks fabulous, and I can spend my holiday getting it shipshape first.'

'You could run it as a B&B,' suggested Amber, as usual eager to provide a solution or a plan for every problem. 'Put in a swimming pool and a cabana, get one of those lovely wooden outdoor hot tubs and charge a fortune. And you could provide gourmet breakfasts, you like mucking around in the kitchen. Those bedrooms are all large, so you could put in king-size beds and smarten up the décor, make it five-star.

It's a fabulous house and the gardens are amazing — great photo opportunities all round.'

'I don't know if it would be viable. The council tax alone on a property as valuable as Thornhill, and the insurance isn't something you take on lightly. And heating that house costs a fortune too, not that it needs to be heated all the year round and you can turn off the radiators in individual rooms, but still. And the garden takes a lot of time to look after — trust me, I know! I was my grandmother's garden slave for years - it's not like looking after your average suburban back yard. You'd probably need to have a very high rate of occupancy to make it work financially.'

'How big is the place? I haven't been there for so many years — would it be about an acre?'

'Two acres of garden, I think I remember and a few acres of fields - you know, the one where the glasshouse is, the field beside that one and the flower meadow. And then there's the copse behind the fields, remember how we used to call it "the forest". I wonder if the swing is still there in the oak tree, I must have a look. The forest is another three acres, I think, so it's probably ten acres in all.'

'Amazing! And I forgot to say — I'm having a few friends over for our wedding anniversary on Saturday night, why don't you come along? You know at least half of them, and they'd love to catch up.' She made a face. 'Torsten and I were going to stay at a lovely place in Truro this weekend to celebrate, but that's all cancelled with him being away, so I thought I'd have a little party all by myself instead.'

When Miranda went up to her room, she spent a long time in a hot shower in the luxurious bathroom, deeply immersed in thoughts about Thornhill, her parentage, and her grandparents. Wrapped up in her hotel bathrobe she sat in the nearly dark room and looked out over the town, where she could just see the Norman towers on the cathedral backlit by the floodlights at the front. Ever since she left Donna's office, the idea of living at Thornhill and getting a job in Exeter had hovered in the back of her mind.

She might do it, but not as a B & B, that would never be part of the plan. She would have to get a top-level job nearby first, and maybe she could have a couple of people come in and share the house with her and pay rent. It probably wouldn't be necessary, because she thought she would be able to live there and cope on the interest from the invested money and what she earned. There must be some firm in the vicinity that could use an engineer of her kind, but she would never again take a job that didn't interest her. The first thing to do was to try to work out how much the interest income would come to per year. Her mental calculation took some time, but once she had deducted what the approximate income tax on the income might be, she concluded that it might be possible. Close to fifteen thousand a year, she said out loud, so it might pay the Thornhill costs and I would have no rent to pay. I could probably do it, but would I really want to look after that huge garden?

Chapter 4

The next morning Miranda stopped outside the gates at Thornhill and decided to leave the car there rather than push the two elaborate wrought-iron gates open and drive in. The smaller man-gate on one side, as her grandmother called it, squeaked when she opened it, and she made a mental note to bring some oil next time. Walking up the gravel drive overhung by oak trees on one side and with a wide expanse of lawn on the other, she noticed how much the weeds in the gravel had grown since her last visit and made a mental note to check if there was weed killer in the garden shed, so she could spray the drive before going back to Bristol. She studied the house with fresh eyes as she approached and thought of Amber's suggestion that Thornhill would make a lovely house to run as a B&B.

How would it appear to someone coming to spend a weekend here?

She stopped where the long drive curved around the big circular rose bed and tried to see the house from an outsider's point of view; a large and solid looking two-storied house built of rectangular blocks of honey-coloured Bath stone. A symmetric façade with pillars on both sides of the front door, five tall multi-paned windows each side of the door and the same on the second story with an additional window over the front door. The house was a perfect copy of many Georgian buildings in Bath with clean lines, classic Tuscan plain pillars without fussy capitals and a shiny black front door, wider and taller than modern doors.

It *would* appeal to visitors, she decided, it's quite impressive and the fact that it's so deep or whatever you call it you go upstairs and there is that long passage right down the length of the house in both directions from the central staircase with rooms on both sides, it's much bigger inside than it looks from the front. And the garden is lovely when it's kept tidy, and look, some of the roses are in flower already, but the weeds! Talk about knee high, I'd better get my gardening gloves on, and the grass looks a lot lusher than it did just three weeks ago. I wonder which day the lawn guy comes.

She walked up the three shallow steps and unlocked the door and even after a year of being empty, the house felt like it always did. Every time she opened that door she was home again. The high-ceilinged hall with the wide staircase straight ahead that branched into two halfway up, the open gallery at the top and the way the light fell through the windows each side of the front door and cast a grid pattern on the black and white tiled floor, this was her home. Could she really bear to sell it and never come here again? She walked through the ground floor rooms and checked that everything looked all right and gradually realised that in the back of her mind she was also studying furniture and rugs with the eyes of someone looking for what might need updating or replacing. Upstairs everything was tidy and just the way she left it when she came back from New Zealand after her grandmother's accident, when she spent a couple of weeks sorting things out, but now it was a lot dustier. She returned downstairs and headed to the kitchen for a glass of water.

I'll take my glass and do a tour of the garden, she thought, as she let the tap run for a minute to avoid drinking water that had sat in old pipes for weeks, but as she turned away from the bench, she noticed something and stood frozen to the spot. There were four breadcrumbs just to the left of the basin. After a moment she reached out and touched one and it was not dried and hard, but semi-soft and it stuck to her finger when she pressed down. She smelt it and knew it was very fresh, no older than a few hours.

How was this possible? The garden man didn't

have a key to the house, Donna had said she hadn't been here for ages, the front door was locked, all the windows were shut and none of them broken.

She left the glass on the bench and checked the pantry window and the side door that exited the house from the hallway between the kitchen and her grandfather's study. There were no unlocked doors and no open or unlatched windows. Which left the basement. She went down the stone steps into the cool dark corridor that ran the length of the house and opened every door: boiler room, laundry, cool store, carpentry room, the old coal cellar, the big space her grandfather called the junk room but found nothing amiss.

Back in the kitchen, she drank her water and considered the options. She could call the police, but what would she show them? Four crumbs? Or more correctly, three crumbs now. And nothing else to show that anyone had been there, and nothing seemed to be missing. But if someone had used the kitchen this morning, she thought, they must have left some other trace. Was there a hidden stash of food somewhere? Surely nobody would bother to enter the house just to eat a sandwich.

It took only a few minutes to find it. She opened every cupboard and every drawer, and when she pulled out the deep bottom drawer in the column of drawers next to the pantry she found the answer. Instead of whatever her grandmother used to keep there, it now contained someone's supplies: a loaf of sliced bread, a jar of peanut butter, three tins of soup, a can opener, two tins of sardines, a packet of crispbread, a jar of coffee, eight small cartons of long-life milk and a packet of Weetabix. In the drawer above it were the utensils needed for one person, a small saucepan, some cutlery, and a couple of plates, mugs and bowls. She recognized the cutlery and the plates; they had been borrowed from the other cupboards and it made perfect sense. That's what she would do, too; keep everything she needed in one place, clean up and put things back, never touch anything else. Very organized, take all the things you need from one place and return them to the same place.

Miranda sat down at the long kitchen table and looked across at the two open drawers and tried to make sense of what she had discovered. She had found nothing else that indicated someone lived here, but would somebody really come in just to eat? Whoever ate here must sleep here too, but where? Everything had seemed very tidy when she did her round, nothing disturbed anywhere in the house and there was nothing left out on the bench, the basin was dry. There was a bit of water in the electric jug, but there was no way of telling how long that had been there. There was nothing missing anywhere that she could see. It was so carefully done, only those four crumbs and those two bottom drawers, and who would even check them if they just came in to have a quick look around. She started a more thorough search and found a slightly damp tea towel draped over the enamel bowl on the bottom shelf under the basin.

Half an hour later she knew a lot more after returning upstairs and searching all the bedrooms more thoroughly. The intruder was male, and he used the smallest bedroom at the end of the left-hand hallway upstairs, which was a good choice for a squatter. It was next to the narrow uncarpeted servants' stairs that came out at the end of the passage by the kitchen. There was no built-in wardrobe in that bedroom, but inside the large oak cupboard she found shirts and two pairs of jeans in the hanging space, along with a navy-blue fisherman's jumper and two pairs of shoes. A storm jacket hung on a hook beside the trousers. In the narrow drawers on the side were underwear and socks, a torch, spare batteries, a cell phone charger and a Kindle. She turned it on and found that he had forty-three books loaded, a few novels including "Life After Life", which was one of her favourite books, and a lot of books about archeology, design and history.

And once again his strategy made perfect sense, she admitted to herself, as she stood there with his Kindle in her hand, deep in thought. This room was perfect, he would hear anyone coming up the gravel drive, he could see if they headed for the front door, then race down the kitchen stairs and into the basement or out the side door. And if a visitor went to the side door, he would have time to run down the main stairs and out the front door, so he was a strategic thinker. The only disadvantage was that light might show at night, but only somebody coming up the driveway would be able to see it, and the curtains were thick and lined, so probably nothing would show from outside anyway. Nobody driving past on the road could see the house at all, the driveway was far too long, and the trees hid the house. He was obviously clever, so he probably went outside and checked if the light was noticeable. The bed was made under the bedspread, but it was so tidily smoothed out that you couldn't tell by just looking, and the bedspread was folded under the pillow just like in all the bedrooms, like Gramma always did.

She knew now which bathroom he used, but when she did her initial round, she hadn't noticed the towel behind the door and not opened the cabinet under the basin, so she hadn't found his shaver and toilet things. Now she knew quite a lot about him: he was an educated, intelligent, adult male and very tidy. Either quite an unusual young man or someone a bit older, her guess was a bit older. He was also good at covering his tracks and very detail conscious, probably a serious kind of man.

She left Thornhill with a plan developing in her mind, so deep in thought that she arrived back in Exeter without the slightest memory of having driven through Shillingford St George. As she drove towards Machine Mart she told herself she couldn't tell anyone about this. It would sound crazy to most people, but she was so intrigued by this tidy squatter that she wanted to find out more. There was something strange and unusual about a man like that being squatter. The sort of man she imagined he was, who would probably normally never consider doing this. Getting into an empty house and living there, goodness knows for how long. And why? She only needed to buy a few things, because there were sets of all basic tools in the Thornhill basement, though she was sure there wasn't an electric drill. The old one had died and Gramma would never have replaced it. And she must call British Telecom and get the phone line re-connected, the sooner the better, so she would do that from car park. She had no idea how long it would take to get that done, but if it was a slow process she could ask if she could borrow the Iridium Go from work, which could live-stream via satellite, but getting it set up might be quite a production and she didn't want to go back to Bristol to fetch it.

Chapter 5

At Machine Mart an older man helped her select the best cordless drill for her purpose. 'Drilling holes inside a dark cupboard,' he said, unsurprised by what she told him she wanted to do. 'Get a small Black & Decker, like this one here. It's a reasonable price and the battery is OK, and it has a keyless chuck which makes it quick and easy to change to a different sized bit. This model has LED lights at the front too, so you can see what you're doing.'

'Perfect! Let's have that one.' Miranda took it out of his hand and put it in her basket. 'I also need white cable clips for holding the cord against the wall, and then could you tell me which aisle the CCTV cameras are in? Oh, and I need a roll of gaffer tape.'

The helpful assistant went with her from aisle to

aisle and made sure she found exactly what she wanted. He was slightly puzzled by some of her questions in the CCTV aisle, but a quick foray on the internet on her phone provided the answer.

'This one,' she said and held up her phone. 'I need one I can connect to this excellent app I've just loaded on my phone, so I can monitor it live.'

They parted on the best of terms, her assistant having only slightly dented her opinion of him by making a remark about how surprising it was to find a woman who knew so much. But she excused him based on his age and thought that men like him still working in this kind of shop made things so easy. Men who thought a woman needed guidance and help and went out of their way to provide it.

Half an hour after she entered the shop, she walked out the door, threw the bags on the back seat and set out for Thornhill again. In her head she rehearsed what she would say, if the man was in the house when she got there. He might, of course, return while she was there, but if he came up the main drive, he would see her car and probably turn around. He could also come in through the forest behind the meadows at the back and take her by surprise. Her guess was that he was out during the day and only spent nights there. Surely it would be too risky to stay there in the daytime when someone might come, or when the mower man might spot him through a window. But there was no knowing what he might do, so being prepared seemed like a good idea.

Once again, she stopped outside the big gates, closed the car door quietly and walked towards the house, keeping an eye on the window to the small bedroom at the corner without being obvious, but there was no sign of life. In the hall she stopped with the door open behind her, stood very still and listened for what seemed like a full minute, but there was no sound apart from the wind in the trees along the drive. She closed the door behind her as quietly as she could and engaged the lock catch, so she could get out by just turning the door handle. Quickly and silently, she walked to the end of the passage to check the side door, then through all the ground floor rooms, and last of all upstairs. But when she was one room away from the bedroom the unknown man used, a sudden thought stopped her. What if he was there now, maybe asleep? She tiptoed forward and peeped in, but the room was empty, so she returned downstairs to pick up the two bags she had left by the front door.

Looking around the kitchen she considered the plan she had made in the car. The phone socket and a power point were at the end of one of the long workbenches, the cord from there to the modem must be as unnoticeable as possible, so running it up the corner and in through the bottom of the overhead cupboard would be easy, and from there it could continue inside the cupboard to the top, so her visitor didn't spot the modem if he opened that cupboard for some reason. Walking around the kitchen she pictured where he would stand to make a sandwich and to use the stove, and which chair he might sit on at the table.

I bet he sits with his back to the window so he faces the door to the hallway, she said quietly to herself, that's what I would do to avoid being taken by surprise by someone approaching, from either the side door or the front door. So, if I'm right I'll get good views of him both when he's at the bench and when he's sitting at the table, not full face but good enough. And I'll see his face as he moves around, fills the electric jug or washes his dishes – a good opportunity to study him and try to figure out who he is, what type of person he is, apart from obviously a reader, and tidy and strategic.

It took forty minutes. She put the camera and the gaffer tape inside the cupboard and drilled a hole though the bottom, right in the corner, then in one the shelf inside. She climbed up on the benchtop and drilled the final holes into the highest part right up against the ceiling. Putting the drill down she mounted the camera with silver gaffer tape in the angle formed by the ceiling, the side of the high cupboard and the wall. She climbed down from the bench and stood back, satisfied that a cursory look around the room wouldn't alert anyone, moved to a different position and considered.

'Right,' she said out loud. 'Let's say that he stands by the bench and makes a sandwich, and then he turns around to head for the other side where the jug is, like this and his eyes pan around like that... and no, I don't think he'll notice it, his focus will be lower, what a good thing the ceilings are so high. He *might* spot it, but it's not likely, and if he does, by the time he climbs up and pulls it down, I've already got him recorded and saved – unless he spots it tonight. Maybe I shouldn't have mounted the camera today, but it's done now, I'll take the chance. Tomorrow I will come back with the modem and connect it to the phone line, and the job is done. Amazing what you can get done super-fast, if you find that the guy you are talking to, went to the same school and had a crush on you. I'll do the rest tomorrow.'

She smiled at the memory of her call to BT from the Machine Mart car park. After being directed to a local representative the conversation with someone called Pete had gone exactly as she had expected with no chance of getting things done in a hurry, until he asked for her name and the address, when suddenly anything at all was possible, and the call turned into a ten-minute session of reminiscing and catching up. They had ended up making a date for a drink when he left work that night, and he promised to bring the modem. Sitting through a trip down memory lane over a drink seemed a small price to pay for instant service. Shameless and opportunistic, she thought now, but it would also be interesting to see what Pete had turned into. He had been rather non-descript at school and she had never known him well, but maybe he had improved and become more interesting.

Back at the Mercure Hotel Miranda decided she had no time for a late lunch. She must get tidied up for afternoon tea with Mrs. Wylie who was due at three. It felt surprising to think that she had been flat out since nine that morning and only just got back in time. Going back and forth between town and Thornhill and getting the things she needed in town and then climbing around in the kitchen, not to mention tidying up after herself. She smiled at the memory of how careful she had been not to leave a single particle of sawdust on the bench for the squatter to notice.

Miranda was looking forward to seeing Mrs. Wylie again, and then she would meet Pete at a bar near his work for the promised after-work drink, followed by dinner with Lilian; the day had become a marathon of activity and people.

She tied her hair up in a ponytail and went down to the foyer to wait for her old science teacher to arrive for afternoon tea. Apart from the three years she had spent in Wellington, they had met regularly since she left school. At high school, when Amber was focused on nursing as a career from age thirteen, Miranda had no idea what she wanted to do and changed her mind every couple of months until Mrs. Wylie became their science teacher. By the time she was in her final year at school and trying to decide exactly what science courses to take at university, Mrs. Wylie had become her favourite teacher and remained the mentor who helped her sort out her university study options and encouraged her to take extra papers simply for the sake of interest and variety.

When Mrs. Wylie arrived, Miranda was shocked by her appearance and hoped her face didn't reveal her feelings. Her old teacher's face seemed to have sagged since she saw her last, and she was pale with dark circles under her eyes.

'You look great, Miranda,' said Mrs. Wiley, as they sat in the lounge with cups of tea and scones. 'Are you staying here? I haven't been her before, but I like it - it has a very comfortable feel to it.'

'The rooms are good, too – I stayed here when I came for the funeral, and as I'm here for a week this time, I decided to make it a real holiday. I could have stayed at Thornhill, of course, but the temptation to avoid shopping and cooking and making my bed and then tidying the house up when I leave was irresistible. How are you?'

Mrs. Wylie smiled. 'Getting better, definitely feeling better. I'm sorry I couldn't be at the funeral, but I was having my last chemotherapy treatment that day. I've got a type of lymphoma cancer, but they might have got on top of it – let's hope so.' She smiled at the concern on Miranda's face. 'I'm seventy-six, you know and I'm lucky to live in an age when these things can be treated. But tell me about your work? What kind of company is it?'

They spent a couple of hours talking about Miranda's job and the one she had in Wellington for three years and reminiscing about other students and teachers. Miranda was, as always when she met up with Mrs. Wylie, impressed by the way she kept up with everything, new science developments, old students' marriages and babies, and everything in between. When Mrs. Wylie said she had sold her little house and moved into a modern apartment, Miranda very nearly confided about the squatter at Thornhill, but she pulled back at the last moment. Something like that might be too intriguing not to share, and the last thing she wanted was to have it talked about. Miranda accompanied Mrs Wylie to her taxi and watched Mrs. Wylie being driven away.

I'd forgotten that she doesn't drive, she thought, and these days she might not feel up to riding her bike like she used to. She always arrived at school on that upright blue bike of hers with her briefcase sticking up out of a wire basket hanging off the handlebar and her hair in a mess, like someone out of a novel from the 1950's but with all the latest science at her fingertips. What a lovely woman she is! I must remember to tell Amber I saw her and that she's been ill, she might not know.

She walked to The Fat Pig to meet Pete at six, and within minutes thanked her lucky star that she had a dinner date with Lilian to use as an excuse to leave after only an hour. Pete was as eager to please as he had been as a teenager and apart from getting quite a bit heavier, he looked much the same as he did the last time she saw him, about ten years earlier. He had heard about her time in New Zealand from Amber, who looked after him when he was in hospital a year earlier. 'She was so lovely,' he said, beaming at Miranda. 'She told me all about your job in Wellington and what you were doing. But what are you doing now? Where are you living?'

She soon understood that he hadn't heard about her grandmother's accident or her death, and he thought Miranda was in town for a quick visit. Though was a shame to use it as an excuse, she let him continue in the belief that she was only there for a couple of days. Quietly amazed that it didn't occur to him that needing to reconnect the phone line at Thornhill must mean that nobody had been living there, she left after a fairly boring hour with a box containing a wifi modem and an assurance that the line had been "priority connected".

Chapter 6

Miranda woke to a grey and windy Wednesday morning, with dark clouds that threatened rain. After deciding on a strategy while she had breakfast in her room, she left just after nine, guessing her squatter would have gone for the day by the time she arrived at Thornhill. Last night she had ended up having dinner on her own, after Lilian cancelled their date in the last minute, due to a toddler with a tummy bug.

'I wish I could come,' Lilian had said on a note of annoyance mixed with humour. 'I'd do nearly anything to get away from one more squirt event, it is truly disgusting, but I can't. Grant is so sensitive to nasty smells that he gags, and the two of them making a mess together is too much to contemplate. I'd turn around in the door and walk straight back out again.'

During her lonely meal Miranda had avoided looking abandoned by having her Kindle propped up against the vase on her table, but she wasn't reading, she was having an imaginary discussion with her dead grandfather. Ever since he died nearly ten years ago, she had done this whenever something needed to be worked through, or when she had a suspicion that she might be making a wrong decision. So last night she imagined sitting in the armchair across from the desk in his study, just like she did innumerable times when she was a teenager. She pictured herself telling him what she had done, and what she was planning to do, and how he would react.

'You must report it,' he would say. 'The man is an intruder, and he could be dangerous. Call the police right away and ask them to evict him. You can't seriously mean that you're thinking of going into the house again and risking him being there! What if he attacks you?' And she would say, 'I don't want to report him, Granda – he is tidy and clean and clever in a smart way. The way he'd organized his belongings proves that, and there were no weapons anywhere that I could see. And he's a reader, he reads good books. I want to watch him, it's so intriguing to think someone's living there in secret and I want to find out why.' And Granda would look very serious and say, '*Anything* can be a weapon, Mirrie - anything! What if you surprise him in the kitchen? A kitchen knife can be a weapon or a bread board. There's nobody around, nobody would know you are there – please don't do this, darling!'

There was nobody at Thornhill, and no sign that anybody had been here since she left yesterday afternoon. If she didn't already know that somebody lived in the house, she might have spent the day there and never suspected it. Leaving her damp jacket on a hook in the cloakroom off the front hall she went upstairs, still with the bag in her hand and found the bedroom just the way it was yesterday, but the jacket was no longer in the wardrobe and the blue shirt had gone. She ran down the kitchen stairs and unpacked the bag on the bench, lined up modem, cable and cable clips. A quick trip to the basement achieved two goals. She checked the washing machine and confirmed her hunch that this was where he put his laundry until he washed it. 'Ten points to me,' she said to herself, 'that's exactly what I would do too.'

In the workshop she found a small hammer and then she was ready to start and half an hour later the job was done. The cable ran in a neat straight line from the socket up the right-angle corner, secured by three small white cable clips, and disappeared into the cupboard. Very neat, he won't notice, she thought, it fits into the corner so straight and so snugly, and if he does notice, he'll think it's been there all along. And if he looks in the cupboard, all he'll see is the cord continuing up through the shelves. He would have to climb on a chair to see the modem on the top shelf.

She returned to the hall and opened the security app on her phone, logged in and set up the link to the modem, using the manufacturer's QR code and password. And suddenly, there it was, the empty kitchen with the chair she had stood on directly below the camera. She walked back down the hallway, looking down at the phone as she went, and then she laughed – she was watching herself walk into the kitchen. It took only a couple of minutes to tidy up and restore order, then she ran down to the basement with the hammer, picked up her jacket and left.

A sudden feeling of urgency made her hurry down the drive towards the gate, prompted by the thought of how annoying it would be to meet him coming up the drive now when she had just finished the final task of what she set out to do. As she drove away, she felt her shoulders relax; now it didn't matter if he came back. She admitted to herself that it was important to observe him first, to make sure he was the kind of man she thought he must be and not be forced into a situation where her only choice would be to tell him to leave. She was tempted to cancel her dinner at Karen's tonight, but she knew that confronting the intruder tonight, after only watching him for an hour or so would not be sensible.

Closer to town the rain got heavier, and her plans for today no longer seemed enjoyable. Instead of a walk around the old medieval part of town and along the quay with lunch somewhere on the way, she spent a couple of hours at the Royal Albert Memorial Museum, surprised to find that her memories of school visits have left her with a completely mistaken impression that it was a dead and boring place. When she came out the rain had turned to a light drizzle, and she stood for a moment undecided about what to do with the car. The clouds were thinning fast and a slight glimmer of sunlight filtered through, so she left the car where it was and walked away down Queen Street. Bella Italia was a lure hard to resist, because she loved Italian food, but she ignored the temptation and continued to the High Street. When she returned to the hotel at the end of the afternoon she was pleased with her day and sat down at the little desk in her room to check the way to the house Karen and James bought last year. It was in a part of town she didn't know well, and she entered the address in Navigate on her phone, so she would find it easily, but at five Karen sent a text to say that Amber would pick her up at half past six.

With nothing better to do, Miranda sat on the bed and watched the last half of a film she had already seen on Sky, and it wasn't until the film ended that she remembered the camera at Thornhill and opened the camera app on her phone. And there he was, standing at the kitchen bench under the window, making himself a sandwich. A tall man, with untidy dark hair and broad shoulders. He left the sandwich on a plate and got a can out of the bottom drawer, then a pot. He was having soup and bread for dinner, and Miranda wondered which soup it was, then she saw the tin he put to one side; it was the potato and leek soup. She sat up straighter, what was he doing now? Getting something out of his bag, which she hadn't noticed on one of the chairs. Aha, he had bought some cheese and biscuits. She smiled and wondered if he had a bottle of wine somewhere. It was like a film but happening right at that moment, and it was an odd feeling to sit there watching him while he had no idea he was being observed. He left and returned with his Kindle, and she got a really good view of his face as he walked into the kitchen. A strong, handsome face, probably about forty, and fit looking. Not a criminal, she thought and then she laughed at herself. What did a criminal look like? Could she tell? But she felt certain that a dangerous or criminal person would not heat up a can of potato and leek soup and make a sandwich. They'd probably have take-out food, something that required no care, McDonald's or fish and chips. She had noted how carefully he put the top slice of bread on the bottom one, lined them up precisely – like his clothes and his drawers, very tidy. She never saw he put between the slices of bread and suddenly she really wanted to know, so she went to her laptop, where the footage was saved via her phone. Starting before the moment when she first saw him live on her phone, she watched him come into the kitchen and go straight to the drawer, get the bread and a plate out, then a knife and – there it was! He turned and got a little packet out of his bag on the chair and opened it carefully. Slices of ham, she thought triumphantly, he made a ham sandwich to have with his soup. But going back to the live feed to watch him eat seemed like one step too far, an intrusion into his privacy, and though she knew this was a contradiction, seeing that the house was hers and he was there illegally, she closed the app and got changed, ready to be picked up by Amber.

'I didn't know you were going too,' said Miranda and did up her seatbelt. 'This is so nice - it will be like those weekends we used to have, when us three girls stayed at your house and sat around and talked all night.'

Amber turned to looked at her and shook her head in mock sadness. 'No, unfortunately it won't be at all like that. Because Karen's tedious husband will be there, of course, and maybe his sister too - and wait for it, possibly *her* tedious husband!'

'Oh no! Really? I can't even remember James very well, I haven't seen him since they got married, just before I went to New Zealand. I never had a proper conversation with him ever. Is he really boring?'

'Let me put it this way,' said Amber and frowned at someone cutting in front of her at the intersection. 'If you like economics and financial analysis and the consequences of some not yet implemented law change to the tax system – no, in that case James is not at all tedious. He is positively riveting. But if those things don't light your fire, you'll be hoping he chokes on his food before the meal is half over. And Karen can't stop him, she just lets him take over and bore the knickers off a room full of people. Torsten *can* stop him - it might be the real reason I married him – he's got that useful knack of finding just that perfect point to interrupt really boring people and change the subject without causing offence.'

'Gloom and doom!', said Miranda, reverting to one of their teenage phrases of disgust and laughed at Amber's talent for exaggeration. 'What is wrong with the sister's husband, then? Another economist?'

'No, but he's a golf fiend – if he takes the floor, we could re-live any random GPA match from the last twenty years or so in excruciating detail, stroke by stroke or whatever it's called in golf. But don't worry, my plan is to get those two sitting opposite each other, or next to each other at one end of the table, and they can battle it out between them while the rest of us ignore them and talk over and around them. Trust me – I've been here before. And I do love Karen, of course!'

The next day was warm and mostly sunny again and at the end of a leisurely morning of shopping, Miranda ran into an old school friend whom she hadn't seen since she went to university, now a mother of twin toddlers.

'Let's have lunch together,' said Lisa when they had caught up on each other's lives. 'My ma-in-law looks after the boys at our house every Thursday from eleven, so I'm free until four. It's my sanity break.'

Their lunch turned into a three-hour marathon of surprisingly interesting conversation and time flew, until Lisa suddenly looked at her watch and exclaimed, 'Oh God, I must run! See you next time you're down,' and disappeared at a run.

. . .

That evening Miranda once again parked outside the Thornhill gates, but this time she drove around the last bend with only parking lights on, did a three-point turn and left the car pointing away from the house, ready to drive back down to the main road. She had another debate with her grandfather on the way there and conceded that however much she felt she was right about this, being prepared cost nothing. She must admit it felt slightly different coming here this late in the dark, but the squatter hadn't got home until quite late. She had kept an eye on the app on her phone while she had dinner at the hotel and left with her shopping bag of supplies as soon as he appeared and she had finished her meal. She smiled to herself when she remembered how he appeared. The way he got in was a surprise, which she knew she should have worked out, but she had overlooked it.

She locked the car and stood for a moment with the carrier bag in her hand to let her eyes adapt to the dark. The sky was perfectly clear now, and the stars seemed impossibly close. The man-gate swung silently open, and she smiled. No squeaking hinges now; she had remembered to bring a spray can of CRC when she came to install the modem. She walked silently along the grass edge of the drive and scanned the front of the house from side to side. There was no moon and despite the stars the night was so dark that she could only just make out the outline of the house, but if there were a movement, she would spot it. If for some reason he came around the house from the back, she wanted to see him, before he saw her.

On the front step she stopped, put the shopping bag down and got her phone out. Standing close to the door with the phone right up against her body, she hoped the light from the screen wouldn't be noticeable through the windows beside the door.

He was sitting at the kitchen table with his Kindle, he had finished his dinner and pushed his plate to one side and now he was reading. The light was on over the long workbench under the windows, and he looked like a man in a painting, a composition of greys and browns. The angle of the camera was perfect, and though she could only see two thirds of the kitchen, she got a very good view of him at the table. She studied the scene for a couple of minutes; the dull light, the man's broad shoulders silhouetted against the light behind him and the slight glow from the Kindle vaguely lighting his face. His dark hair was tousled as if he had just pulled something roughly over his head, and he sat utterly still, totally engrossed in what he was reading. She turned the phone off, slid it into her back pocket and unlocked the door, then slowly turned the curved brass handle. Leaving the shopping bag, she pulled the door nearly shut behind her and crossed the tiled floor to the passage leading to the kitchen. Her trainers made no sound as she crossed the dark hall and there was no ambient light, but she knew every inch of the house and could walk through it blind-folded without bumping into things.

She stopped in the half shadow between the dark corridor and the dimly lit kitchen and waited for a few moments to marvel at the stillness of him, then she took one step forward and said very quietly, 'Hi, I'm Miranda.'

She had rehearsed this greeting, tried to make it casual and friendly, as if she was introducing herself to someone in a social situation. He didn't jump, as she had thought he would; he just looked up and stared across the space between them. She stayed where she was, unmoving with her hands hanging down her sides, as if to say 'look, I'm not a threat' and after a moment he got up, but he remained beside the table.

'I'm Felix,' he said simply and waited.

Miranda now felt quite certain that he posed no danger. His face was calm and despite the thoughts that must be circling in his head, his stance was relaxed, so she walked forward, put her phone on the table and said conversationally, 'I know you're living here, and I worked out how you got in. Please sit down.'

'I'll leave,' he said. 'I can leave right away.'

'No, you can't – how would you carry all your clothes? That bag you have is nowhere near big enough.' She said it even though it was a rather silly thing to say, but she hoped it might defuse any tension he felt.

He studied her face, as if he was reading a map of an unfamiliar landscape that he knew nothing about but must suddenly navigate safely. A woman who calmly turned up and seemed to know things about his life in this house. Who was not threatening him or even annoyed, and who wasn't frightened of being alone in the house with a stranger.

'You're quite right – it's not big enough. I've bought some more gear. I'd have to put some things in shopping bags. I have a couple.'

She liked his deep voice and the way he studied her face before he replied, the way he assessed her – just like she had assessed him.

'How did you know how to get into the house?'

He didn't answer, his eyes didn't even flicker sideways towards the pantry door and Miranda said. 'Never mind, but I worked it out.'

He made no reply, but she could see he didn't quite believe her.

She smiled. 'Yes, I *did* work it out. This is my house and I know it pretty well - I grew up here.'

'Ah,' he said again, nothing more.

'Why are you here?'

'I'm ... homeless.' He sounded as if he were surprised that the word could apply to him, as if he had only just realised. 'I really am, I have nothing apart from those things upstairs - and a bike.'

'You don't have to leave. I'm not going to live here right now - you can be my tenant.'

He gave her a wry smile and said decisively. 'No, I *can't* be your tenant! I mean what I say, I am homeless, and I have *nothing*. At the moment I'm saving to be able to rent a bedsit or something, but I haven't got quite enough yet – everyone wants a month's rent as a deposit and then a month's rent in advance. I've just started a job but it's not permanent, so I can't rent this house. I must leave.'

Miranda thought how odd it was that she wasn't in the least frightened of him, she felt as if she knew him, and the uppermost thought in her head was that she must make him feel secure, make him see that she wasn't a threat and that his situation was not hopeless. A strange instinct and the irony of it was not lost on her. She was alone with a strange man at night in a house way out in the country, but she felt he was the one who needed reassurance. She pulled out the chair opposite his and made her movements relaxed, her voice casual.

'Do you mind if we talk about this over a glass of wine? Do you drink wine? OK, good – let me get the bag I left by the front door.'

Lights, she thought, and reached for the hallway light switch as she walked away and then further on the one for the ceiling lights in the front hall. We need some normalcy here, no more sitting around in a house that's in total darkness apart from one very weak light in the kitchen. We're not hiding now - this is a house that's in use.

When she returned with the bag, he had put his plate and glass on the bench and was standing in the middle of the kitchen, puzzled and slightly wary.

'Did you call the cops?'

Miranda put the bag on the table and said indignantly, 'What!? *Of course*, I didn't call the cops! Why would I do that? You're not going to harm me, are you? And you haven't stolen anything that I've noticed.'

She walked around him and took two wine glasses out of the glass-fronted cabinet over the far bench, put them on the table and started taking things out of the bag: the wine bottle, the Camembert, the wedge of blue vein cheese and the box of crackers.

'Can you get a plate out of the cupboard above the dishwasher, please?' she said without looking up and sat down at the table. 'And there's a corkscrew in the second drawer from the top beside the fridge.'

He put the plate and the corkscrew on the table and remained standing. She glanced up at him, noted the puzzled expression and smiled. 'Would you please sit down? You're too big to hover over people like that, it's like having a cliff looming over you. And perhaps you can pour the wine while I get this organised?' She gestured at the things in front of her and started unwrapping the cheeses.

He did what he was told; sat down, opened the wine and poured it into the glasses, then got up again and walked around the long table to put hers beside her. Nice, thought Miranda, he didn't just push it across, I like that. He still has that puzzled look on his face. He doesn't know what to make of this, and he's wondering what it's going to lead to. Well, who knows? I don't.

'And why are you homeless?' she asked without looking at him, while she cut cheeses into wedges and slices. 'I hope you don't mind me asking, but it's relevant, I think.'

He was silent for a moment, and she looked up with a question on her face. He ran his hand though his thick hair and made it stick up even more, and Miranda smiled; it was a touching gesture. He hesitated, then he said slowly, 'I was … scammed, defrauded. I've lost everything.'

She heard the desolation in his voice and saw the reined-in sadness and tried to observe him without staring directly at him. The thought that he had been living here alone, probably with minimal lights on, moving through the silent house like a ghost, was intolerable and she felt indignant and angry on his behalf. Nobody should be so lonely when they were struggling with loss, any kind of loss. But she must get some details, so she could work out what needed to be done, because someone must help him, and she had appointed herself to the task without any conscious thought. She trusted him already and he needed her, even if he didn't realise it yet, so she must work it out. She put the plate with cheese in the centre of the table.

'Listen, Felix – if it isn't too much to ask, I'd like the full story. I think you owe me that. And I'd like to hear it without having to drag every single word out of you. Have some cheese and drink your wine and tell me what the hell happened! Because I really want to know.'

'It's a long story.'

'So? I've got all the time in the world, I'm here for another three days. The only reason I'm not staying here at Thornhill, is that I couldn't be bothered cooking and shopping for food and tidying up when I leave, so I'm in a hotel in Exeter. And I'm catching up with a lot of old friends, so not having to drive back here at night after drinking wine makes things easier too. Who scammed you?'

'My partner. Our house burnt down, and everything was lost. She took the insurance payout and disappeared.'

'Wow!' said Miranda, before she could stop herself. 'Sorry! I didn't mean to sound so excited, but that's pretty dramatic. Did she have a lover or something? Do you know where she is?'

'Yes and no.' He picked up a cracker and a piece of cheese. Oh, good, thought Miranda, he's going to eat some cheese, next he might have a drink of wine and this will feel a bit more normal, nearly social, which will be good for him. I can see how he has isolated himself and what it's done to him, it's heartbreaking!

'If you want the whole sorry saga, I'll tell you', said Felix. 'Erin and I had talked about separating. I knew I'd made a big mistake because she wasn't the kind of woman I could live with forever, and I wasn't the right man for her either.'

He paused, then said thoughtfully, as if it had only just occurred to him. 'I think it must have been lust, but I mistook it for love.'

He looked into the middle distance, silent for a moment and then he sighed. 'She did have a lover, as you said, or I thought she did, but I couldn't figure out who it might be, not one of our close friends anyway or I would have picked that up. And I knew she was bored with me, she made that very clear. When the house burnt down, which happened while I was away overnight seeing a client, I thought it was a genuine electrical fault that caused it. And so did the fire service and the insurance assessor, it seemed pretty straight forward. They pinpointed the starting point of the fire inside the wall behind the panel heater that was hard-wired into the wall in the living room and there was no reason to doubt it. There was a heavy curtain just beside the heater and once that burst into flames things happened fast, the fire reached the ceiling and spread from there and that was it.'

He drank some of his wine. 'This is nice, I haven't had this one before. I must remember it, for when I can afford to buy wine again.'

'And?' asked Miranda, who wanted to hear the rest of the story. She was pleased with how normal his comment about the wine was. He was loosening up, not looking as if he might walk out into the dark night and disappear. 'How did she get away with the fraud, or the theft I suppose it was?'

'I think I'd better start by telling you the things I've found out afterwards. Erin had it all planned, she must have prepared very carefully over a long time. One of our neighbours who lives diagonally across the street, told me later that she'd seen a guy with a van the day I left to visit the client, the day before the fire. I was away overnight - the client is in Northumberland. The neighbour couldn't see the man's face because he was wearing a cap, but she said he reversed up to the open garage and she watched Erin come out and give him a hug, and then they both carried a lot of stuff out, some of it in boxes. So probably she was making sure that her favourite clothes and jewellery were out of the house – and her laptop. Possibly other things too, paintings or ornaments, there's no way of telling what she took and what she left. It was a two-story house and once it had collapsed on itself it was ... well, just a pile of burnt rubble.'

Miranda was fascinated and then she felt guilty and hoped her face hadn't reflected her feelings. 'I'm sorry – again! – it seems rude to feel that this is exciting, when your life is ruined, but it is like a thriller or a film.'

'I wish it were.' He sighed. 'The fire started the next day, at lunchtime – I was still in Northumberland, just about to fly back, and Erin was at work. We moved into the spare room at a friend of Erin's and started the process of claiming the insurance and so on. When the money came through, it went into a separate account we'd set up for the purpose, separate from our other bank accounts. I tried working from our friend's place at first, but it was hopeless, they had two little pre-school kids and a dog and there was no peace or quiet – not for a moment. So, after a while I had to give up on that. Then a colleague lent me a room in his office, just for a month while someone was on holiday. I'd had my laptop with me on my trip, but my desktop computer and the two big screens went up in flames.'

'What do you do?'

She drank some of her wine and watched over the edge of her glass as he lifted his glass too. Good! she thought and waited until he put it down, then got up to top both their glasses up. We need to become friends now, I must make him trust me, so I can do something about this. I simply can't understand why he's ended up here, in this state. Was there nobody who could see what was happening to him? Some kind of break-down, a loss of confidence and motivation – whatever it was, it's kind of paralyzed him and put him into this fatalistic state, where he seems to feel he is powerless to change anything. And what are the police doing about it?

'I'm an architect,' he said, 'and I worked from home before the fire. For a month it was good, being able to work from my friend's office. I had somewhere quiet to work and they let me use their CAAD program, which was vital, of course. I don't have the full CAAD software loaded on my laptop, only the bit you need to show clients things. Thank God I had the habit of backing everything up at the end of each week on an external hard drive. It was in my laptop bag when I went away – or things would have been a real mess.'

He picked up another piece of cheese, and she noticed again that he gradually seemed more animated, less closed-up. He looked at her across the table and she thought, my God, his eyes are such a startling blue that I can see it even in this low light, and that black hair, it's unusual, maybe he has Scottish blood or DNA from the Spanish armada, maybe Cornwall?

'Anyway, a few days after the insurance money came through, I was going to buy a new computer, and I went online to transfer some money from the insurance account into my personal account – and there was only a balance of a few quid. It had all been moved the previous evening to a new account that Erin had set up in another bank - and from there she had moved it to an account in the Cayman Islands, which took a bit of work and quite a while to find out. And she had disappeared, of course, as of that morning. I've never seen her since.'

Suddenly he sneezed and then again and got to his feet. 'Sorry, I'll go up and get my antihistamine pills or I'll be sneezing all night. I'll be back in a moment.'

Miranda sat quietly speculating about where this was going to lead, and she knew exactly what she was going to ask him when he returned.

Chapter 8

Felix returned with a pill in his hand and swallowed it with some wine. 'I hope this isn't going to make it useless. I just remembered I never took it when I got home – I meant when I got back from work.'

Miranda let the self-correction stand; she knew why he said it. 'Had you told her you were going to buy the computer the next day and that you'd transfer that money?' She was trying to come to grips with how Erin could have known to move the money just in the last minute. 'I can't understand why she did it just then.'

'I think I took her by surprise – she wasn't expecting me to use any of it right away. But I mentioned that I was going to buy a computer, we talked about it over dinner. She must have had it all sorted out in her mind ahead of time, how to do it, account set up and waiting, everything – she was all ready for the get-away. So, she acted right away.'

'I wonder why.' Miranda stared into the middle distance, deep in thought. 'I mean, she might as well have transferred the money *after* you bought the computer – why was she in such a hurry?'

He nodded and lifted his hands in the age-old gesture of "who knows". 'I've thought endlessly about how it all happened and what motivated her to act just then, and the only thing that occurred to me was that she thought I would transfer the entire balance to my business account, not just what I needed to buy the computer.' He sighed. 'But anyway – when I discovered the money was gone, I called Erin's phone and it was offline, so I rang her office and they said she had resigned a couple of weeks earlier. She'd probably spent that time getting everything organized. And as I said, I've never seen her since. She didn't come back to the people's place where we were staying, she just vanished.'

'Have you managed to locate her?'

'No, she simply disappeared, literally without a trace. And her friends, the people we were staying with, they swore they knew nothing, but I didn't believe them – or let's say, I didn't believe that Janet, the wife, knew nothing. I told her I thought she was lying and moved out that day. At that stage I had enough in my personal account to rent a room for the time being.'

He stared into the distance again before he continued, and Miranda didn't interrupt.

'I felt so demolished, demoralized – as if I'd failed. I couldn't bear to ask for help or approach friends. Everyone thought I was living with some other friend - I just avoided meeting them or having conversations. I was in a strange place and now I don't understand what I was thinking at the time. I'm not due for a progress payment for either of my current jobs for a while and my money soon ran out. I didn't even have a car - it was in the garage at home when the fire started. I had flown to Manchester and hired car there. I was on the verge of starting work on two new commissions, but things got complicated when I had to leave that borrowed office. My professional insurance would only pay out under certain circumstances, and because everything that was lost in the fire had already been claimed on the house insurance and that money was gone, I was stuck. I couldn't claim for the computer and the software and I didn't have loss of income insurance. It was a real Catch 22 situation. And then I came here.'

He's just pouring it out, all in a jumble, thinks Miranda. The poor man, he's not talked to anyone about this, he's been living in this bubble of lonely misery for weeks. It's awful, and I was right before, someone *does* need to help him, or this will destroy him.

'Why did you come here, I mean to Exeter?' she

asked instead of commiserating. The important thing now was to not let him continue reminding himself of the days and weeks after his life fell apart, to take a step forward from here. We need to move on from this harrowing topic, and then start planning and reassuring him.

'I just wanted to get away, somewhere smaller, easier to get around, away from people who pitied me and gossiped. I've always liked Exeter, so I got on a bus and came here – I really don't know why. But rents were surprisingly high, and it took a while to get a job – I thought I might run out of money. I heard about this gorgeous house and how the lady who lived here was in a coma and that the house was empty, had been empty for a long time. Just idle gossip, but I asked a few questions and then rode out here on the bile I bought to check it out.'

'Where did you live? I mean, where was your house that burnt down.'

'In Bristol. I moved there when I got together with Erin. Her family lives in Wales, but she had worked in real estate in Bristol for several years before we met, so it made sense to live where she knew the market, so to speak. And before you ask, her family know nothing either – I've asked them more than once.'

'So you found a job here?'

'I'm just filling in for someone who's on two months leave – or it could be a bit longer.'

They sat in silence for a while; Miranda was thinking, and Felix looked down at his wine glass. The house was very quiet, and she realised that she had never sat here in such total silence before. She got up, flicked on the light over the second bench and switched the fridge on. When she turned back, his eyes were on her, once again puzzled.

'What a good thing it was that I left the power on,' she said cheerfully. 'I did it in case I wanted to come and spend a weekend here. You'll need the fridge, so you can keep your food fresh. I don't know why you didn't turn it on before.'

He just looked at her, with an unspoken question, and she knew he was finding it incredible that she was going to let him stay in the house.

'Oh, and we'll go down and turn the boiler on before I leave,' she continued, 'so you have hot water, and so you know how it works. There's a separate system for the hot water, it won't turn the central heating on. It all runs on diesel and the tank is full, it will last until next winter. The phone line was re-connected two days ago, and there's a wifi modem in the high cupboard up there.' She pointed. 'If it turns out that the wifi covers the whole house or at least the ground floor, I'll leave it up there, though it's a funny place for it. You can use my grandfather's study, just across the passage from here – there's a big desk in there, but feel free to rearrange it, so you can work here when that job in town finishes. If you don't have to spend your savings on rent, you could buy that CAAD software and use it on your laptop.'

'You must be mad!' The stern look he gave her reminded her of her grandfather, and nearly made her laugh. 'No, really - you don't even know me!' he said seriously. 'You are too naïve, too trusting. I could be lying, I could be a conman or anything at all, how would you know? I might have made it all up. Maybe I murdered Erin and I'm on the run. And I've already told you I can't pay rent – and you could let this place for a fortune.'

'But I'm not about to let it – that's not in my plan, whether you're here or not. You can live here, no rent, just look after the place. And if you like gardening you could do some weeding perhaps and spray the weeds in the shingle on the drive? Do something therapeutic out in the fresh air instead of hiding indoors. It can't be good for you to live like this.'

And get some kind of normality back into your life, she told him silently in her mind, and stop living in self-imposed imprisonment. Aloud she said, 'And of course, I trust you! You're reading Life after Life – only good people read books like that.' And then she laughed at herself. 'Well, there's probably no research to prove that theory, but it sounds right. I'll give you a key, so you don't need to come in through the ice-cellar.'

'You are a very unusual woman! How did you

figure all this out, and why is the modem in the high cupboard and – well, why everything? I never saw any sign that you'd been here, but you must have because you know what I have upstairs.'

She poured him another glass of wine and told him how she discovered someone was living there, when she saw the breadcrumbs on the bench.

She smiled at the memory. 'So, when I had to drill holes through the bottom of the cupboard and up into the top shelf to get the cord from the phone socket up there for the modem, I took great care. I swept up the sawdust and wiped any marks off the bench, so you wouldn't notice.'

He turned to look up to where she was pointing, then his head swung towards her fast, and she knew he had spotted the camera.

'Ah!' he said and started to laugh, and his entire face was transformed. 'How long have you been watching me?'

A laugh! thought Miranda triumphantly, trying to look casually amused, as if she had expected nothing else. He laughed! When he smiles his whole face changes and when he laughs, I want to laugh too. What a lovely guy he is – he must be saved!

'Only a day and a half, I just wanted to observe you for a while before I came. I mean, you could have been someone dangerous, but I felt sure you weren't any kind of threat. I thought the kitchen was the best place for the camera. I wasn't rude enough to put a camera in your bedroom — I draw the line at voyeurism. But I must confess that I've been through everything in your bedroom, checked what type of person you might be, what you read, looked in the drawers. And I figured out that you came in through the ice-cellar, because I saw you leave this morning, you disappeared into the pantry and didn't come out again until this evening. There's only one way into the pantry from the outside, seeing the window is nailed shut, but I didn't know that door was unlocked.'

'I really don't get this,' he said, very serious again. 'How you dared come here at night, on your own, and just walk in! You're the bravest girl I've ever met and totally reckless. But to get back to that ice-cellar, I'm really interested in it. I've never heard of one like this, like a passage. I suppose the house was built in the late 1800's? I knew it wasn't an original Georgian house, because it seems to have been wired for electricity from the outset and there's a toilet that looks antique in the cloakroom off the front hall, but not one of the very earliest types. A lovely thing to have in a house like this. But the ice cellar as a direct link into the house is very unusual, maybe unique.'

Miranda nodded. 'I know, but my great-great-grandfather - I think that's the right number of great's — the one who built the house, he was an inventor and an innovator. That's how he made his fortune. He had a pile of patents for various mechanical things to his name and he was quite well-known in his day. There's a story about him in a book in the study, a book about the family. People said that he couldn't look at anything without working out a better way to construct it. And he spent years working away in some horrible shed he rented down by the river in Exeter while he was trying to make his first really good invention work – and he slept there too. Then, when he was finally making money, he got married to his childhood sweetheart and it was all up and up from there. That's why there's that big room in the basement we call the woodwork room. He made all kinds of things down there, both wood and metal things, he never stopped experimenting and inventing. I don't know if you noticed the two antique lathes, one for metal and one for wood? He must have been an interesting man.'

She picked up the last piece of camembert and put in on a cracker and licked her fingers. 'He drew the plans for the ice cellar - we still have the drawings in the study. He made the ice cellar long and narrow and deep and then he had them line it with stone blocks, and he decided to build that little hut as an entrance with two doors, like an airlock. Did you notice that the inner door is heavy? It's triple layers of solid wood to stop the heat coming through into the cellar itself in the summer. And the other end of the ice cellar is the same, of course, first one thick door, then a space and then the steps up to the little door into the pantry.' She drank some of her wine and thought he looked fascinated, so she continued. 'So, the iceman would drive his cart up to the hut, unload the big blocks of ice and slide them down the chute beside the steps, and they'd pack them in straw or sawdust, or whatever it was they used. This would happen in the early spring - the ice must have come from some ice warehouse somewhere. The hut is on the cold side and shaded from the midday sun by the house itself.' She smiled at the memory that had just come into her head. 'It was my play cave when I was a small girl. To open that door between the banks of shelves in the pantry and turn on my torch and go down the stone steps into that cool, dark tunnel – it was like a magical world. Did you know straight away what it was?'

'When I first biked out here, I scouted around for a while, and I came back three days running, checked that nobody seemed to come and go and looked for a way in. I saw the coalhole, but that was thoroughly nailed up. I never saw anyone apart from the lawn mowing man who was here one day, so I went away again and came back later. I put little bits of twigs in the cracks of the external doors, and they hadn't fallen out, so I assumed nobody came into the house, at least not often. I didn't realise to start with that the little hut was actually an entrance into the house, and then to find it wasn't locked – that was lucky. And it's interesting that the ice box is still in there, I hadn't actually seen one apart from in illustrations.'

'I think it was taken out of the kitchen in the 1920s or 30s when they got an electric fridge. Think of the job they must have had getting that old contraption apart and down into the ice-cellar, the tunnel isn't very wide. God knows why they didn't just scrap it. I used to pretend the zinc-lined box for the block of ice was a swimming pool for creatures who lived in the ice-cellar. I put water into it, one jug at a time and put some of my dolls in, dressed up in leaves, so they'd look like underground fairies, and I was allowed to have candles down there too – well, nothing could catch fire, could it?'

'You were a very lucky little girl,' he said. 'And there are still a couple of candle stumps on one of the stone blocks on the side, they might be yours. But tell me, where is the video streamed to from that camera?'

Miranda grinned and picked up her phone, opened the CCTV app and pushed it across the table to him, 'Here we are, you can watch me watching you watching us – live-streamed in real time. And it gets saved on an external hard drive attached to my laptop in my hotel room.'

'How do you know how to do all these things? Is this kind of thing what you do for a job? Or are you just a natural surveillance expert?'

'I work for an engineering company.' For some

reason she didn't quite understand, she downplayed her role. 'I know how to find these things out. At first, I thought it would take ages to get the phone connection up and running again, because it usually does – BT isn't the fastest telecom in the world, I don't think, so I was thinking of all kinds of complicated ways of streaming the data to my phone or laptop without it. I nearly asked if could borrow the Iridium satellite device from work. But the guy I talked to about the phone connection turned out to be a friend from high school, so it got done quick smart.' She didn't mention that she had to go on a date with Pete to get the job done.

It was very late when she left, and the wine bottle was empty. They had been in the basement where she gave Felix a quick lesson about the boiler that heated the water. As he walked her to the car and Miranda got her car key out she suddenly remembered. 'Oh no, I forgot to show you. There's a key to the front door on a hook in the cloakroom off the front hall. It's just inside the door, beside the coat rack, take that! And if you can figure out a way to close off the ice-cellar door, the outside one, that would be great.'

'Of course, I'll do that tomorrow.' He looked back at the house where the front door stood wide open with a broad river of light streaming out over the steps and the circular drive. 'Thank you! You are very generous and trusting. I don't know how I'll ever repay you.'

'I'll tell my solicitor that I've got a tenant, but it's none of her business who you are or if you pay rent – just so she knows someone is living here if there's any gossip. And I'm going to pretend to everyone that I've known you for ages in Bristol. It's nobody's business that we've just met. Come and have dinner with me at the hotel tomorrow night, so I can tell you what you need to know about the house, it's got a few quirks. And you can tell me some more about the scam. I'm dying to know why the police wouldn't do anything when you reported your wife for arson and theft – we never got to that.'

She looked in the rear mirror as she drove down the driveway towards the road. He stood outlined against the light spilling out from the house and watched her drive away, and the thought that he could now go back into a house with lights on pleased her. She knew her instincts had been right, and she had never been able to do anything so dramatically life-changing for anyone in her whole life.

Chapter 9

Friday already, thought Miranda, when she woke up. Look at the rain! On the other hand, it's an incentive to stay inside and do some research into the fire that ruined Felix's house. And she must ask Amber what she should bring for her party and email Donna about her tenant. It would probably be better not to call Donna, or she might ask all kinds of questions Miranda didn't feel like answering.

Downstairs at breakfast she picked up a copy of the Exeter Daily that someone had left on the next table, and though she only intended to glance through it, she found herself going through it, page by page, and within minutes she felt she belonged here again. News about local events, businesses and sport, and familiar names in various contexts combined to create a sense of belonging here that she hadn't experienced since she left Exeter. An article about her old high school mentioned teachers who had taught her and sports competitions she had taken part in.

It's not just the local content, she thought, and looked at the rain streaming down the window beside her, it's the way it reconnects me to people and places, I can nearly feel it drawing me in, like something I didn't know I was missing until just now. I don't suppose I've read the Daily since I left for the job in New Zealand four years ago, and before that I was at university in Bristol and I hardly ever bothered with the paper when I came home. I don't think I read a single issue on my visits to Gramma after the accident.

Thoughtfully she folded the paper and returned to her room and started a search for a house fire in Bristol with immediate results. Within minutes she was reading an article, where a spokesman for Avon Fire and Rescue was quoted as saying, "it was an explosive fire that caused significant structural damage to the two-story house within a short space of time, possibly due to the gas-fuelled hot water system". She made a few notes on the pad she kept in her laptop case and considered what to try next. When room service knocked on her door, she took the laptop, retreated downstairs to the lounge and ordered a coffee, then took up the search again. And then, in the middle of reading another short article about the fire, she had an idea that she felt certain her beloved Granda would totally disapprove of, and she could practically hear the words he would have used to tell her not to do this. Disregarding his advice she looked up the number for Avon Fire and Rescue and called them on their non-emergency number.

'Good morning,' she said breezily to the person she was directed to. 'My name is Miranda Carlow. I'm a journalist with an engineering background. I'm thinking of writing an in-depth article about the risks associated with gas cylinders, particularly about their placement. Someone told me about the fire in Clifton last year where a house suffered serious structural damage and actually collapsed - and a large gas cylinder used for water-heating purposes seems to have contributed to the destruction. Can I ask you a couple of questions, please?'

Twenty minutes later she put her phone down with a thoughtful frown. Her pad was covered in scribbled notes and her mind swirled with ideas. She turned the page and started two new lists; questions to ask Felix and things to tell him.

The email to Donna was short and she saved it to send right at the end of the day, because she knew that Donna didn't read work emails in the weekends, and she wanted to be back in Bristol before Donna responded. For some illogical reason she felt that distance would make it easier to brush off any probing questions. Donna had known her since she was a little girl and might appoint herself in *loco parentis* which would be intolerable. There was just the slightest hint of this when they met in her office, and it must be avoided at all costs.

Donna,

Thank you for all you've done for me since my grandmother died. I do appreciate all the trouble you have gone to. Just a quick note to let you know that I already have a tenant for Thornhill — a friend from Bristol, incredible coincidence! He's working here and wants the house for a year. I will move some personal things into the lockable 'butler's pantry' off the kitchen before I leave. I've had the phone line reinstated and installed a security camera, and I can't think of anything else that needs doing. I will inform the insurance company that the house has been let and is no longer empty. Please tell the garden man to continue to mow the lawns and to send the invoices to me. I have downloaded a basic tenancy agreement from the Law Depot — I know my tenant well and don't wish to be too formal.

Kind regards, Miranda

But at least I know what his surname is now, she thought, thanks to those articles. How funny that I never thought to ask him. Am I being careless, or are my instincts super perceptive? And no way am I going to lock things in the butler's pantry. Fancy him not turning the fridge on because it would add to the power consumption, he said he felt guilty enough over his use of the stove and the washing machine! There's something about that guy, he's either the calmest, most transparently trustworthy man I ever met - or else he is a fantastic actor and capable of convincing me of anything he likes. Either way this whole thing is more interesting than anything I've seen on TV lately. I want to find out more about him, I'll do some research.

Felix Huxford's life turned out to be an open book available to anyone who typed his extraordinary double-x name into a search engine. There was one article about him being dux of his school twenty-two years ago with a nice photo of a tall, gangly boy (another x thought Miranda and giggled), another about Felix winning first prize in a county tennis tournament for under 19s, then one about him getting a scholarship to the University of Bath, and so it continued. He had won an award for innovative eco-friendly house design, and she found links to articles about modern style changes and sustainable house design he had written over the years. She delved further, but he seemed to have no presence on social media. His private practice had a website with photos of his designs and a short bio, but no content other than his articles on eco-friendly housing. It was minimal both in content and appearance, light grey, dark grey and very pale green; uncluttered and striking.

A waiter came past and picked up Miranda's coffee cup and she realised to her surprise that it was nearly lunchtime. On an impulse she texted Amber: *Are you working, or would you like to join me for lunch at the hotel? M xx.*

Within a minute Amber replied: *I must be at hospital at 2.45. Will be with you at 12.30.*

Just before Amber arrived, Miranda had another idea and ordered flowers to be sent to Donna on Monday at her office, so they would arrive after she read the email about the tenant. This gesture seemed to combine being gracious with putting a neat full stop at the end of Donna's involvement in Thornhill. I'm getting quite strategic, thought Miranda, as she watched Amber coming towards the entrance, perhaps I'd make a good detective – or a politician.

Lunch with Amber was always fun; their meetings, even if far apart, were so easy. They effortlessly picked up wherever they had left off and reverted to shared jokes, old favourite phrases and school slang, they knew each other inside and out. Amber had been on a diet most of her life and Miranda knew exactly what would happen when they ordered, a ritual they had gone through many times. They sat near a window and the persistent rain created an endless pattern of runnels, that Miranda saw out of the corner of her eye like a slight interference in her concentration.

'Do you get distracted by things you see out of the corner of you eye?' she asked and Amber looked up from her study of the menu, slightly disconcerted, and said, 'I don't think so – do you?'

'Frequently!' Miranda laughed. 'Like what I just spotted at two o'clock over your shoulder – don't turn around, he'll know we're talking about him.'

'Oh dear, you know it's fatal to tell me not to turn around!' Amber moved her head from side to side. 'My head is trying to turn and have a look, and I can hardly control it.'

They grinned at each other because this had been a standing joke since they first met. One of them would say 'don't turn around now' and the other one would nearly always turn.

'What are you going to have? How about the sole with Bearnaise sauce? You like fish. They serve it with the tiniest potatoes rolled in butter – delicious!'

'God, no!' said Amber. 'What are you thinking? You know that I'm not eating anything with lots of fat and carbs. I'll have a look at the salads, or maybe an omelet and a salad.'

Twenty minutes later Miranda looked at Amber, across their two plates of sole with Bearnaise sauce and buttery potatoes. 'It's a pity you can't have a glass of white wine with the sole – such a nice wine, too, but I suppose nurses have to stay sober. But tell me, what can I bring to your party?'

'A bottle of wine or perhaps crackers and pate, or a dip? It's just a very simple party and the main meal is all planned. Georgie offered to do the dessert, so we know it will be cheesecake, and Harold is doing a potato gratin with onion and something. Or you could bring a man?'

Miranda laughed. 'I don't have a man locally – not that I have one anywhere else either. I haven't managed to get serious about anyone since I got back from New Zealand. And the Kiwi didn't last, he found that absence didn't make his heart grow fonder, quite the opposite, it made him ravenous for change. And who is Harold?'

'Tilly's new boyfriend, or more correctly, Tilly's only boyfriend ever. I'm beginning to wonder if she hooked up with him because he can cook – she's pretty useless in the kitchen and it appears he's a food maestro.'

As soon as Amber left for work Miranda went back to her room, and suddenly she couldn't wait a moment longer to start searching for Felix's wife. The rain was easing and way over to the west the cloud cover was breaking, promising another lovely spring day tomorrow. Just like yesterday, she told herself, a promise of better things to come, which I hope is true for Felix too.

She googled the name from the article about the fire, Erin Lloyd, and found multiple links to house sales and a photo of Erin that had clearly been photo-shopped for publicity purposes, because the next photo was from Facebook. Four people at an outdoor table, having drinks and Erin was not quite so slim or smooth looking, but very pretty and sexy in a busty way. Ha! thought Miranda, I bet she thought clients wouldn't notice that other photo was edited or taken ten years ago, isn't that false advertising? And then she told herself she was being judgmental because she knew that Erin was a criminal, or at least she had been told that Erin is a criminal. It was, of course, possible that Felix was the criminal, and that he was hiding from the police by living invisibly at Thornhill. But she remembered his face when he said he was homeless, and she couldn't believe anyone could fake that forlorn look of pain and sadness, and the desolate twist of his mouth when he told her he had lost everything.

It surprised Miranda how easy it was, slightly surprising that all she did was type 'Erin Lloyd Bristol' into the search bar in Facebook and instantly found the right person, but probably helped by Erin's helpfulness in putting Bristol as her home town, which had made finding her much quicker.

There were no privacy settings on Erin's page, and she scrolled though photos and posts for half an hour, gradually getting a grip on her and Felix's friends. After another half hour she was getting somewhere; she found a photo of a line-up of people dressed for the races with Erin next to an unnamed man. If you looked carefully, you could see that his hand was resting on her backside, and her shoulder leaned ever so slightly against his upper arm. That's a dead give-away if I ever saw one, thought Miranda, that speaks of lust or new love. That's how people stand when they're first in love, or in love forever – that sort of 'I can't resist touching you' thing. She copied that image and some others that she gradually came across to her hard drive and then into a Word document. When she closed her Word file, she had eleven photos.

She went back to the top of Erin's Facebook page and noted that the last photo was posted two days before the fire, a picture of a slice of what looked like chocolate cake and a cup of coffee on a round marble table. Above the image Erin had put, "I promise never to eat cake again – haha!". In the background was a doorway to what might be a hall, and to the right of it hung a painting of a snow-clad peak, or maybe it was a photo. Miranda looked at the image of the cake for a long time and tried to imagine what could possibly have been in Erin's mind when she posted that photo. She was planning to burn down their house, had probably already removed all she wanted to keep to a safe place, and was also planning to defraud her husband and leave him destitute. And then a lighthearted photo of a piece of cake? And why that heading? She could only wonder if Erin was conveying a final message, to be decoded by others, or if she simply posted it because that's what came into her head at the time, with no particular meaning.

But Erin was such a planner, so would she really do something so spontaneous and random? So meaningless? Miranda continued to look at the photo while she pondered, and then she saw something unexpected, nearly unnoticeable. At the extreme bottom edge of the picture, just under the marble tabletop was a man's knee and hairy thigh, without trousers, possibly without underpants. Christ! thought Miranda, here's a daytime photo of Erin having coffee and cake with someone who's taken his pants off, and it was broad daylight, you can see the sunshine reflecting off the far side of that table, and she's eating cake and about to commit arson! She saved the photo and adds it to the others in the Word file.

Chapter 10

Felix arrived at six carrying a black storm jacket with a hood and found Miranda in the bar, where she had told him she would be when she sent a text that afternoon to reinforce her invitation. 'Please come and have dinner with me,' she wrote. 'I've eaten alone a couple of nights and I think we should get to know each other a bit better. And I have thought of a few things I want to tell you and I actually made a list. Come at six if you can and we'll have a drink first. I'll wait in the bar.'

'Is it raining again?' she asked when he put the jacket on a spare chair. 'I thought it had cleared up.'

'Didn't you see me with it this morning? I had to go back into the ice-cellar to get it – I left it there last time I came back in a downpour. Today I left through the front door for the first time, it nearly made me feel like a normal person.'

'I haven't looked at that app since we looked at it together last night,' she said. 'It never occurred to me. I'll delete it and close the link. I'm not going to spy on you.'

'No, leave it! It's a good security thing to have, even if that's not why you put it there.'

They ordered drinks and Miranda tried to decide how to bring the subject of Erin up without upsetting him. But her quandary sent a signal that he picked up and misunderstood. 'Have you changed your mind? I understand completely if you have. It's a crazy situation and you don't know me.'

'I think I do know you,' she said slowly and tried to smile. 'But I'm not sure how you'll react to what I'm going to tell you - you might get angry, and rightly so. But here goes. I did some research today, lots of it. About you and Erin and the fire. I might as well confess a couple of things straight away before I even start. I've invaded your privacy, hacked stuff, talked to the authorities, told people lies and generally behaved in a way that would have made my Granda send me to bed without pudding.'

She held her breath, waited for an explosion, or at least a frown, but he burst out laughing. 'Really? You've done all that in one day? And what did you find?'

'A whole lot of stuff, some of it old and some very

new. And some of it might be embarrassing for you, but I think it's important for you to have all the facts.'

He said nothing, just nodded and waited.

'I found lots of things about you, from your schooldays to the present, all good. And I saw that you're not on Facebook or Instagram, but Erin is – or was.'

'I'm not on any social media, but I'm thinking of it right now actually. As an architect, not as an individual.'

Miranda nodded and lifted the laptop from beside her on the banquette. I want to show you some photos, but first I want to tell you about my talk with Avon Fire and Rescue.'

His eyes widened. 'You've talked to them?'

'Yes, of course - I had to, didn't I? Nobody would know more about the fire than they do. Not that they would tell me anything confidential, but I said I was a journalist with an engineering degree writing an in-depth story about gas cylinders and their involvement in catastrophic fires. Because an article in the paper mentioned the hot water gas cylinder at your house, and that it had contributed to making the fire so explosive.'

'And what did you ask them?'

His intense blue gaze was fixed on her face, and she could practically see him processing what she had said to Avon Fire and working out the significance of the gas cylinder. Obviously, he knew it was there and now he was working through the possibilities in his head. If this wasn't such a damn tragedy for him, it would be fun, she thought, we could be good at this together, investigating mysterious fires, things to do with structures and engineering.

'Last night you said the wiring behind the panel heater had a fault and curtain hung just beside it, and the article said there was already serious structural damage when the fire trucks arrived, so I wanted to figure out how that could have happened so quickly. One eyewitness said she heard an explosion and saw flames coming out through the roof and then it collapsed, so that fire got right up through the roof on the top floor! How the hell did that happen so fast? It didn't seem reasonable to think a burning curtain could have accelerated things to that point in such a short time.'

He made no comment, so she drank some of her wine and continued. 'I wanted to know where that gas cylinder was, how far away from the seat of the fire, and as much about any other facts that I could find out. Because I said I was writing that article, the guy at Avon Fire was really helpful, so I might have to write the damn thing now, because he'll be looking for it and it needs saying, it's good info both for the general public and for companies who install califonts. Mind you, I haven't looked into what the safety regulations say already, but I will certainly do that. But back to the fire. Your house was built in an angle, like the letter L. Two stories on both wings, if that's the right word. The gas cylinder was right in the corner of the L, where the living room angled back along the side of the garden, and the kitchen was right next to that in the other leg of the angle with the upstairs bathroom nearly straight above. So, it was the logical place to have the big gas cylinder, with the flow-through water heating unit mounted on the outer wall. The panel heater was between the corner of the living room and the long window overlooking the garden, and there was a curtain, a heavy linen curtain, lots of fabric, enough to pull right across the window, right?'

He nodded, and she took another sip of wine. 'Don't let your wine get cold! Have a drink. Anyway, where was I   oh, right, the curtain. The guy I talked to said he'd look up the scene photos while we talked, because I asked how they knew there was a big heavy curtain there. He said you can see a deep pile of fluffy ash of some material other than wood or wall lining in the burnt floor structure right below the panel heater, and they thought it could have been something flammable draped over the heater to dry, like some idiots do. But it was the linen curtain, they know how to find these things out. They could tell it was a big mass of linen, because of the big pile of ash-y remnants. They found it when they lifted the collapsed stuff off and could see through the ground floor beams to the ground. So, I asked if the ash heap was under the side of the window or was it really a bit further over in front of the heater – I pretended I thought the curtain might have caught on the corner of the panel heater, you know? And he got really interested and said it looked a bit odd, and perhaps he would have a chat to someone about it - and maybe I'd hit on something.'

She paused and took another sip of her wine. Felix remained silent, but his focus on her was now so intense it felt like a physical touch.

'So, this is how it went, the whole scenario,' she continued. 'The faulty or lose wiring caused a fire inside the wall, the flames came through into the room, the curtain caught fire, then the entire wall and the ceiling caught fire, and the heat went through to the outer wall. The bricks got so hot they heated the cylinder, or bricks might have exploded out of the wall. It's possible that nothing was noticeable from outside, apart from perhaps a bit of smoke seeping out, until that cylinder blew. Burning wall lining would have flown in all directions inside the room, when the cylinder blew its top – because that's what they do, and the gas squirted upward and became a gigantic blow torch, and the eaves got involved and the end result was a disaster.'

Again, he said nothing, so she took yet another sip and continued. 'I think the wiring was tampered with by Erin's boyfriend – unless she's good at that sort of thing herself, and I suspect that the curtain was pulled right back and the long tail of it was draped over the heater, adding mass to the initial fire. Or else the curtain had been taken off the curtain rod and was simply tucked in behind the panel heater and draped over it and on to the floor. Talk about a great start to a fire! A pretty clever scenario for arson. It's even possible that they made a hole in the wall lining for tampering with the wiring. That's what I would do because that way it ensures A, that plenty of oxygen could get the fire started really well inside the wall, and B, that the flames would come out through the hole really fast and the curtain would become engaged, as the fire service call it.'

'Good God!' said Felix, looking a bit shocked. And Miranda looked at his expression and thought, you've got no idea how shocked you might be quite soon, you poor man. I'm sorry to do this to you, but it's got to be done.

She looked regretfully at the nuts in their pretty bowl and decided they must wait; she couldn't talk and chew nuts at the same time. She opened the document she had created with Erin's Facebook photos, which she had copied large enough to see detail well, so there was page after page of full-page photos.

'Come and sit beside me so we can both look at this at the same time. Erin's Facebook page has no security settings, nothing at all, so anyone can see everything. I just copied and pasted these - I didn't actually hack anything, didn't need to. I spent some time studying the photos from social occasions over the last year, lots of them - and some things stuck out. There's a core group of eight or ten people you used to see regularly, not frequently, but you met up with them more than two or three times in that year.' She scrolled slowly down the pages and Felix leaned forward to look more closely.

'This was the first one that caught my attention.' She paused at the row of dressed-up people smiling. 'It's not the only one, but I noticed that Erin is leaning slightly towards the guy on her left, her shoulder touches his upper arm, which could be just a wobble when the picture was taken, or it could be something else. He is not part of your core group of friends, which made it interesting.'

She took another sip of her wine and made the page bigger and scrolled up – now they were looking at the lower bodies of Erin and the man, and it's obvious that his hand is behind Erin's backside. There was a long moment of silence, then Felix said without expression, 'Right, I see. Anything else?'

'Yes, a similar thing in one other photo from the same occasion, too much contact and of the wrong kind and then this significant one.' She scrolled right down to the last image, the picture that was the most recent on Erin's Facebook page. 'Do you recognize this place?'

'Yes, it's the house of some friends of that couple we stayed with after the fire, the guy she was leaning against in that other picture lives there. I've only been there once, but I remember that picture on the wall. We probably only met them two or three times in all. Why is this one significant? Maybe they were thinking of selling their house.'

Once again Miranda made the picture bigger and even before she pointed it out, he spotted it. 'Aha,' he says. 'She was having coffee with Ralph, the guy who groped her.' He scrutinized the picture. 'Can you make that any sharper?'

'Not in the Word file, no – but I've saved these images on the hard drive too, so I could try with the originals. Why?'

She could feel energy radiating out from him now, like a force field; it must mean something, and she began to feel excited.

'Try it now and I'll show you something you might have missed.'

A few minutes later he leaned over and pointed. 'That's sharp enough, can you darken it a bit more? See that? There's a reflection in the glass on that picture on the wall. I could only just see it, very vaguely, before. Look, there's Erin's hand holding the phone a bit out and up to one side to take the picture of the cake on the plate, you can see the line of her arm, there's her head and …'

'Oh, no!' exclaimed Miranda.

Erin was naked; you couldn't see the details, but her nipples were dark and looked like two dots against the pale outline of her body, and the lower curves of her breasts just below the dots were perfectly recognizable. The rest of the reflection disappeared against the lighter areas of the picture behind the glass.

After a moment's thought, Felix got his phone out and texted someone, put his phone down and picked up his glass. 'I've asked the couple we stayed with if they have Ralph's phone number. We'll see what happens now.'

'I'm so sorry,' said Miranda. 'I really am, Felix! I wouldn't upset you for anything, if I didn't think this was relevant. You said you suspected she had a lover, but you didn't know who it was. Are you going to call him? If they give you the number?'

'You haven't upset me - you've just surprised me. Don't worry, I'll live,' said Felix calmly, but there was a tension in his stance that spoke louder than words. 'I don't actually expect them to reply to that text. I told them to their faces I didn't believe that they had no idea where Erin had gone or why, and then I left. I've had no contact with them since, so I'm probably off the Christmas card list now.'

'Let's go in and have dinner. I've talked far too

much and I'm hungry.' Miranda closed the laptop and zipped the case up, but when she looked up Felix was over at the bar talking to the barman. He returned with a determined look on his face, opened his mouth to speak, and she said quickly. 'Yes, I did, and please let me do it! *Please* let's not argue about it! I think life has dealt you a very poor hand, and I've just inherited a lovely house, and I have a very well paid but slightly boring job.'

She picked up her laptop case and studied his serious face and could see that her paying for the drinks was not sitting well with him, so she touched his hand and smiled. 'Come on! Tonight is on me and later on, you can take *me* out for dinner, and I promise to be outrageously extravagant. I'll order French champagne and caviar and some rare kind of roasted bird, hummingbird or something - and it will cost you a fortune.'

She started walking towards the dining room and he fell in beside her, looked down and smiled when she looked up. 'You are without a doubt the most incredible woman I've ever known, or perhaps you're a force of nature ...' And then his phone buzzed with a call and they both stopped.

'Hi,' he said neutrally. 'Thanks for calling back.' A long silence followed; at one point his eyes widened and he started to say something, but the person he was talking to carried on. Miranda could hear the man's voice, but not what he said. Two couples walked right in front of them, but Felix didn't even see them, his entire focus was inward as he listened.

'And when did you find this out?' he asked abruptly, with barely concealed menace in his voice. 'Yes? And what does she know?' After a minute he said goodbye and put the phone back in his pocket.

'I'll tell you over dinner, this isn't the right place. I hope we get some privacy.'

'I'm sure we'll be fine' says Miranda casually. She had no intention of telling him that she personally chose the table this afternoon and reserved it, due to its comparative seclusion.

Chapter 11

When a waiter showed them to the deep alcove, where their table was nearly as private as if it were in a separate room, Felix slanted a sideways look at Miranda as they sat down. 'Another of your initiatives?'

She took the menu the waiter handed her and made no reply. Instead, she said, 'They do fish very well here, they're known for it - and their bearnaise sauce is top class. And sometimes they combine it with things you don't really expect – little food adventures.'

Nothing further was said until they had ordered, but then Felix, once again decidedly serious, said, 'I've decided to pay you rent, not much but what I can afford.'

'Why? There's no need for you to pay me anything.' She tried to sound as if it wasn't important either way, hoping he was not going to argue about it. There were far more important things he should save his money for, but she couldn't say this; she mustn't give the appearance of trying to run his life.

'Miranda, you are being irresponsible!' The look he gave her was so like her grandfather's that once again she nearly laughed at how concerned he was about her actions, despite the fact that they were in his own best interests.

'Did you think of the potential consequences for you if this arrangement goes on for a while? If there's no money changing hands, I might be able to legally claim "squatter's rights" and you'd lose your lovely house. I could change the locks and lock you out.'

At first, she thought he was serious and started lining up the facts about squatter's rights in her head, and then she noticed the corners of his mouth twitch, and they both laughed. 'I thought you were serious! And if you did manage to do that I'd just come in through the ice-cellar and live in my bedroom at the other end of the house - and I'd soon drive you crazy by me leaving the kitchen untidy and not emptying the dishwasher and you'd just leave. You're miles tidier than I am.'

'Probably right,' he said, 'but I've already blocked the ice-cellar entrance. I got up very early this morning and I found all I needed in the way of tools in that workshop in the basement. You'd have to demolish the door now to get in from outside.'

The young wine waiter poured Miranda's wine as if it were a radioactive liquid, very slowly and carefully with a look of frozen concentration on his round face. She waited patiently until he had poured for Felix and left, before she spoke.

'There's one thing I keep thinking of and I simply can't understand it, but I didn't want to ask you before. Now that I've confessed how I pried into your life, I might as well ask you. Just say no, if you don't want to tell me. Why are you not with other friends, good friends that you know well, or family? There must be people in your life, who would have you to stay – who are concerned about you and want to help you.'

He was silent for so long that she regretted asking; this was very personal, and he was struggling to answer. She looked past his shoulder to give him space, out at the rest of the dining room, where tables were gradually filling up, then suddenly she spotted her friend Lilian's sister Rose and her husband, whose name she couldn't remember, being shown towards a table on the far side. Rose gestured in their direction, said something to her husband and came across the room. Oh, bugger! thought Miranda, now I have to introduce him – what terrible timing! She leaned over and said quietly, 'Sorry, someone's coming to talk to me, I'll get rid of her as fast as I can.'

Smiling at Rose she got to her feet. 'What a coincidence – how are you, Rose?'

'Mirrie!' said Rose and kissed her cheek. 'I haven't seen you for years and years, you look amazing.' She turned expectantly towards Felix, who was standing up looking quite relaxed, and Miranda said, 'Rose, this is my friend Felix, who's here on a work assignment.'

Felix shook Rose's hand, and she looked appreciatively at him, then her smile widened. 'I hope you'll enjoy it here.'

She left after a short conversation and a final assessing glance at Felix.

'Sorry about that look,' said Miranda and sat down again, 'She'll be speculating about us now and she'll text her sister Lilian, who was in my class at school and ask if she knows who you are, and on and on. Those two are incurable, they trade gossip as if it's some kind of social currency, which I suppose it is, now that I think about it.'

'I don't mind. People often look you over like that, when they first meet you, particularly women,' said Felix and lifted his glass. 'Here's to Exeter!'

Looking at him over the rim of her glass Miranda thought fondly that his belief that everyone got that looking-over when they met new people, was typical of him. He didn't realise it was because of his whatever-it-is, that unusual quality of self-assurance and calm competence and his good looks; that quality that emanated from him even if he didn't say a word.

A moment later she said on a tone of outrage, 'You won't believe this, and *don't* turn around, but she's just got her phone out, she's texting! I'm glad I'm facing her and not you, at least she can't take a photo of you. I wouldn't put it past her, she was always too cheeky for her own good.'

'About your questions earlier,' said Felix. 'I simply don't have an answer. I don't know what happened to me at that stage. When I look back, it seems mad, an over the top reaction, like panic or a depression. It felt as if my whole life was breaking apart, everything I had worked for was gone, the woman I had thought I loved had not only left me without a word of goodbye, but she had conned me and stolen everything we had. I moved out, I couldn't stay in the house with that couple who were really Erin's friends, not mine, and who were lying to me. I couldn't stand the thought of living in someone's guest room, I needed quiet around me, to be alone.'

He drank some wine, and she could tell how hard this was to talk about from the way he gripped the stem of the glass so tightly his knuckles whitened.

'And then it occurred to me, in the middle of that first night there, in that room I hired, that if Erin had planned her get-away and transferred the money in advance of leaving, then maybe the fire wasn't an accident, maybe the insurance money was the fund for her new future, deliberate. I worked though it in my mind so many times — how she left about six weeks after the fire when the investigation was completed, the insurance company had first paid us a portion for living expenses, and then the balance of the money, and we were just about to sign the lease on a flat for the time being, or so I thought. But Erin had been waiting for the big money to come through. Coldblooded deception, while sleeping beside me every night. I went back to our street in Clifton, don't ask me why, it wasn't as if I'd be able to deduce anything from looking at the burnt-out shell of the house. That's when that neighbour across the street told me about the van that came the day before the fire and picked up Erin's things. I only went to see her because I knew she was the eyewitness who described the fire to the reporters, and I wanted to talk to her. I'd never heard about the van before then, I don't know that anyone in authority had been told.'

He looked down, and his face had that look of desolation again, and without thinking Miranda reached across and curled her fingers tight around his. 'You don't have to talk about it again, I shouldn't have asked you! I'm sorry!'

He looked up and managed to smile. 'No, it's ok, I want to tell you. It's been in the back of my mind ever since that day. I keep thinking of it and wondering if I had some kind of breakdown, a panic reaction or whatever you would call it. Moving in with my brother and his wife, or with my widowed Dad, was beyond what I could cope with just then – I couldn't do it. The endless talking about it, the questions, other people visiting and more talking and commiserations. I wouldn't have been able to cope. And on top of that all my friends kept phoning and texting and sending emails – so I opted out.'

Miranda was close to tears. The thought of how he had felt, how the constant well-meaning attention from those around him had nearly cracked him, and how he had withdrawn into himself and his loneliness. Now that he had told her, she could feel it, imagine herself in the same situation. A tear spilled over and she realised she had been holding his hand all the time he was speaking. She released his fingers and wiped her cheek, and Felix said, 'Please don't cry for me, I'm OK.'

'You're not OK, Felix – I can feel your hurt like an open wound. No, don't say anything, just let me say this. I know it's inappropriate, and you don't know me well, but I would do anything to help you, anything!'

This emotional statement was very uncharacteristic for her, and even as she her herself say the words she was embarrassed, but he said calmly. 'But I feel I know you very well, Miranda – perhaps better than I know anyone else. Thank you.'

And then their starters arrived, and they talked about other things and made everyday comments about the food and the town, until without any introduction Felix suddenly put his knife and fork down. 'That phone call from the friends of Erin's that I texted. He said his wife knew Erin was fucking Ralph – excuse my language – and she knew they were 'going to run away', as she put it. He claims she knew nothing about the money, and when I discovered the money was missing, she didn't dare tell me that she knew who Erin had gone off with. She's had one text message from Erin since, just a few weeks ago, saying nothing much, thanking her for their hospitality but not saying where they were. And he also said Ralph's wife is completely devastated, she had no idea about the affair, but she managed to lock their joint bank account and has started divorce proceedings.'

Miranda felt strongly that they needed to stay off these fraught topics for now and have some normality and calm down. Constantly reverting to his trauma wasn't good for him and she must work out how to do something about it, because it was beyond him to do it. His mental energies seemed depleted, but she would try to create a more normal evening, so she said quietly, 'Let's leave that aside for tonight, Felix. I don't mean that we won't do anything about it, of course we will, but I think what we should do is finish our dinner, enjoy our wine and go for a walk before you ride your bike into the night. I don't know if the cathedral is open at night, or if you've seen inside it already, but it's so lovely and I'd like to show you. Let's not think about this anymore and just have a nice time.'

Outside they discovered that it had rained again, and Miranda ran up to her room to get her jacket and hoped that Felix wouldn't think going to look at the cathedral at night was a boring thing to do. She slipped her arms into the sleeves of her jacket as she walked through the foyer and stopped, he wasn't there! And then she saw him through the glass doors, waiting outside and smiled.

The cathedral stood white and glistening, the façade lit by floodlights and the dozens of carved saints and bishops looked down from their niches where they had resided for six hundred years. The paving slabs on the empty forecourt were wet and reflected the light and there was nobody else there; they were alone in a glistening and luminous place.

'This is the perfect evening to see it – I love it!' Miranda turned up the collar of her jacket. 'I love cathedrals in general, but this is mine, the one I grew up with and it's been standing here for centuries. It's like an unchanging benevolent presence protecting the town. Isn't it beautiful?'

'Very - and I have been inside.'

'Look to the immediate right of the main door.' Miranda pointed and walked closer. 'See the guy in the second tier from the ground, the one who sits with his legs crossed and he's got one hand on the opposite arm, high up? That's my favourite of all those sculpted kings and saints and whatever they are – he looks so modern and casual somehow, the way he sits.'

Felix chuckled. 'He might be an impostor, someone's servant who conned the stone carvers. But there are two things about this cathedral that particularly appeal to me. Did you know that it has the longest uninterrupted vaulted ceiling in the world? One hundred meters. Are you religious?'

'Oh, no, not at all. I was brought up in a neutral kind of space. We did religion at school and when I was six my teacher asked my grandparents if they were sending me to Sunday School, and they asked me if I wanted to go, and I said "no, thanks, I'm too busy". And that was the end of the discussion. I just love churches and cathedrals. Are you religious?'

They started walking again, around the cathedral and then back along the Roman wall towards the hotel. It was cloudy and the rain had stopped, but moisture hung in the air like a veil of mist. Miranda could feel that Felix was back to his self-possessed self again. He radiated confidence and calm and she felt comfortable beside him, as if they had walked through many dark towns together in the past.

'No, I'm not in the least religious' he said after a while. 'But I was brought up in quite a religious family, so I've spent a bit of time fidgeting in a pew.'

'You never told me the second extraordinary thing that you like about the cathedral. We got sidetracked – what is it? The astronomical clock?'

'The earliest image of an elephant in England, carved out of wood.'

'Really? I never heard of it before – where is it?'

'We will have to go back one day, in the daytime when it's open and I'll show you.'

Outside the hotel entrance Miranda stopped and turned to face him, 'Take care on the way home, be careful!'

He gripped her shoulders, held her firmly and kissed her forehead, his lips were warm and soft on her cold skin. 'I will. Thank you!'

She watched until he disappeared from sight. She already missed him.

Chapter 12

The next morning Miranda realised when she was halfway to the nearest off-licence that she never asked Felix if he would like to come to Amber's party as she had intended doing, so she stopped and called him. Today it was hard to believe it rained during the night; the sun was shining and the air seemed extra transparent.

'Hi, Felix – are you busy?'

'I'm on my knees,' he said, and she could tell from his voice that he was smiling, and she smiled too. 'I'm weeding - perfect day for it, after the rain. How are you?'

'I wonder if you'd like to come to Amber's dinner tonight – or party, or whatever it is, but it includes dinner.'

'Who is Amber?'

'She's an old friend from school, my best friend - it's their wedding anniversary. Her husband is away looking after his father's business for a couple of months, so she's just having a little party at home for a dozen people, more dinner than party I think.'

'What's his name?' asked Felix, suddenly interested. 'It's not Torsten Andersen, is it?'

Miranda took several seconds to make the connection and then she burst out laughing, and a passing couple looked at her and smiled. 'My God, that's the job you got, your two months of filling in for someone! I never thought of it, but Torsten is an architect too. How funny! I didn't make the connection.'

'I'd love to come – what can I bring? Wine?'

'I'm on my way to get some wine now, and some pate and crackers – that will do for both of us. I'll pick you up at seven.'

She put her phone back in her pocket and told herself it was ridiculous to feel so happy about saying "both of us" as if there was a stronger connection than friendship between them. She must be careful; she found him not only attractive and sexy, but also comfortable to be with, funny and solid in a way she couldn't define, but the situation would probably not lead to anything. That he sometimes seemed interested could just be a momentary thing, it might not take root and grow. Perhaps he was just grateful to her and enjoyed her company, and she had only known him a couple of days. She refused to allow herself any daydreams, because she had been here once before, admitting that she had fallen in love only to be stared at in embarrassment. Just thinking of Dave conjured up the feeling of humiliation she experienced when she told him. He had been openly amused by her declaration and said he was quite fond of her, but he wasn't in love her, and he never would be. I should never have told him, she thought now, I'll never forget the way he looked first surprised, then amused and embarrassed. Awful! She pushed the memory to one side and continued towards the shops.

When her phone pinged on the way back to the hotel, she put her bags on the ground between her feet and pulled out her phone. A text from Lilian: *Everyone stopped spewing and I didn't get it. Will I see you at Amber's tonight or should we meet for coffee? When do you go back?*

Miranda tilted her face towards the sun and closed her eyes and thought this over. Coffee with Lilian would be nice, they could have a real conversation instead of the fractured kind of chat you tend to have at parties. But wanted to visit Mrs. Wylie before she returned to Bristol the next day, she was worried about her. The thought of leaving Exeter planted a strange thought into her head: 'none of this is real, it's a holiday, it won't last, things never do, this isn't reality'. She opened her eyes and called Mrs. Wylie.

'Hi, it's Miranda. How are you today? Oh, good! Can I pop in and see you later on?'

'Come for lunch, dear. It will be nice to have someone visit, and you've not seen my new flat yet. I can tell you how to find me or you can use Google Maps on your phone. It's right at the far end of Exwick, you turn right into Exwick Road, you know, the first big one on the right after you cross the river and then just sort of follow it around in a big semi-circle and turn into Lager Lane. I'm in 8B - on the second floor.'

With that arranged Miranda texted Lilian: *I'll be at Amber's, going back tomorrow morning, visits lined up today, see you tonight. M x*

Miranda drove to Exwick for lunch with Mrs. Wylie, with a box containing four cakes on the passenger seat and a bunch of flowers. Mrs. Wylie opened her door and there were hugs and exclamations about the cake box and the flowers.

'Four cakes! I'm sure we're not going to eat four - we'll have one each with our tea after lunch and then you can take the other two home.'

She put the flowers in water, and Miranda's offer of help with lunch was declined, so she stood by the kitchen window and watched while everything was loaded on a tray.

'I thought we could sit on the balcony, it's just warm enough now, until the sun goes around the corner. Would you like to go ahead of me through the sitting room and open the door, please?'

The balcony was tiny, just big enough for a little table, two chairs and a very large potted plant. 'I was so lucky to get this flat,' said Mrs Wylie and put a plate with quiche and salad in front of Miranda. 'I was hoping to find something close to nature, seeing I wouldn't have a garden any longer, and this is lovely. And I don't have to do a thing, no weeding or pruning, or lawn mowing - I just enjoy the scenery.' She gestured out over the trees and beyond them, green fields separated by hedgerows. 'Being up high is lovely – you get such good views out here on the very edge of town.'

When Miranda left, she didn't take the two remaining cakes that sat in their box on the kitchen table; she knew Mrs. Wylie would enjoy them with her afternoon cup of tea or after supper. Running down the stairs she wondered how many more times she would come back to Exeter and find Mrs Wylie still alive. There was an air of exhaustion and serious ill health about her, as if her body was gradually getting less substantial. She was the last real link from that generation, at least locally, that tied Miranda to her teenage years. Her Gramma and Granda were dead, and her only older relations are a couple of oldies on her grandfather's side that she couldn't remember ever meeting. And she didn't count her friends' parents, they were all a generation younger and still alive.

Chapter 13

Miranda swept her keycard over the lock on the door to her room and thought she would do some more checking on Facebook. She remembered hearing about this from someone ages ago, so there might be a chance that Erin had her cell phone number on Facebook. She had no privacy settings, so perhaps her phone number would be visible even for people who were not Facebook friends of hers. And if that didn't work, she might be able to get it from Felix somehow, though she wasn't sure of how he would react to her interfering any further. He hadn't seemed worried when she said something last night about how they could do this or they could do that, but it could just have been that he was being polite about it.

But let's face it, she thought, I don't think he's got the stamina just now to start fighting his way through all this, or even if he has any idea of how to go about it. I'm sure a selfie queen like Erin will have left a footprint for me to find her in her new life, even if her current social media accounts have gone silent. Someone's got to help him get his life in order again, and it might as well be me.

Erin's Facebook details included her cell phone number, which might, thought Miranda in an attempt to be fair, have something to do with her job as a real estate salesperson and not just due to general sloppiness. She considered the pros and cons of calling Erin, but that would allow her to simply end the call and never respond to anything from Miranda's number again. No, texting was better, she might respond to a text from an unknown number which she didn't have in her Contacts list. The problem was how to word the message in a way that would entice Erin to reply, and she couldn't imagine how she would explain how she got Erin's number, but a few minutes later it came to her. She would use the real estate connection, of course, pretend to ask for advice or something, pretend someone had mentioned her great talent for finding the right house.

She scrolled through seemingly endless photos and posts on Erin's Facebook page, until she found the right thing in a post from a year ago, a selfie of Erin with a client who took her for a drink, a woman called Penny, who had put a flattering comment with the picture:

'You're a superstar, Erin – thank you for finding our dream house.' This comment ended with five emoticons, three hearts, one smiley face and one glass of champagne. Great, said Miranda to herself, I know how to be this person, easy. Hope they haven't been in touch after that and particularly that Erin has the same number.

After some thought she sent a message she hoped would sound convincing: *Such a surprise! Your agency said you're no longer with them, what a pity. We've got two lots of friends looking for houses and we recommended you! Just so you know! Penny* (sad face, broken heart)

She didn't expect anything to happen quickly and decided to have another shower and wash her hair, which she didn't do that morning. Standing under the stream of hot water in the walk-in shower, she mentally catalogued what she knew and what she needed to find out. She was sure that simply sending a text that reached the person couldn't reveal the location of the recipient's phone. The location could probably only be traced if they replied. But would her own cell phone company tell her where Erin's phone was when she replied, *if* she replied? Probably not, it would need a police request or a warrant. Would the police look into it if she linked it to Erin's theft of the money and the arson suspicion, even though they had no open case regarding it? Could you report someone for the theft of someone else's money? She did have a lot of evidence now, and she could give them the name of the Avon Fire guy she had talked to about the curtain beside the heater. Not to mention the fact that someone saw Erin loading possessions into a van the day before the fire. A mass of details to corroborate a claim of suspected arson, and from there a claim of fraud or theft, but no direct evidence. Having Erin's location would be such a bonus, it would add another layer to all the circumstantial evidence, and the police would be able to question her sooner, instead of spending months trying to locate her.

She was drying herself when the phone sounded a message alert in the bedroom, she ran to pick it up and a glance at the screen made her entire body tingle with excitement; it was from the number she had just texted. Suddenly breathless, she sat down on the edge of the bed, and her hand trembled when she opened the message.

Penny! You must have a new number I didn't recognize it. How are you? I've moved away and given up work. I'm living my dream in a sunnier place and thriving on being loved and adored. (smiley face, heart, smiley face)

Right, that was step one. But where was she? Possibly in the Caymans, where she transferred the money to, but that might have been a safety thing so nobody could get the money back and she could be anywhere. Miranda remembered reading that it took years and cost a fortune in legal fees to get anything back from that kind of tax haven, if it was even possible.

"Loved and adored" – ha! Who said a thing like that in a text? She wondered if Erin would reply, if she sent another message right away. But she had nothing to lose and it was worth a try.

I'm sooo envious! Let me guess – Portugal, right? Got a guest room? Haha. (laughing face, palm tree, sailing boat)

And much to Miranda's surprise the response to this came flying back immediately.

No, try again!! You can't come yet, but we're in the process of buying a house, so maybe in a couple of months? Gorgeous house, you'd love it, tennis court, huge terrace with lap pool, triple garage, five bedrooms, just divine. E xxx (house, heart, palm tree, glass of champagne)

Miranda tried to think of another inane comment, but before she had time to refine her ideas, another text arrived.

AND – here's the bonus, when we get sick of sunbathing nude on our terrace, we'll only have a ten minute walk to a gorgeous town with dozens of fab cafes. Bliss! #marblestreet (winking face, sun, heart, champagne glass)

This is where it stops, thought Miranda. Erin is either drunk on wine or drunk on her successful fraud and her new life and she can't resist bragging about how wonderful her life is. And she carelessly added that hashtag that must mean something, maybe a place with a marble quarry, like that town in Italy where marble gravel covers every path. Perhaps she misses not being able to talk to her UK friends and relishes the opportunity to tell someone how great her life is.

Miranda replied to Erin saying once again how envious she was, but now she must run, as she was going to be late for an appointment. She put the phone down and went to her laptop and entered "marble street" in the search engine.

"Alicante, the coastal jewel of Spain, famous for its fabulous promenade paved with 6.5 million marble pavers and lined with palm trees."

Miranda, still wrapped in a bath towel, sat staring at the screen as if mesmerised. She could hardly believe it, this was way too easy, but it couldn't be anywhere else. She wondered if Erin and her man had assumed new names, and could you really buy property in Spain without authentic documentation? Or did they have false passports too, did Erin have a Spanish bank account in a false name and could back it up with a false passport? Was that all part of a plan she had worked on for so long, spent months preparing and establishing a new identity? Those things must take time, even just to find out who to get in touch with for a false passport; how long would it take to do that? Not forgetting all the other preparations, the bank account in the Caymans, for example, a massive undertaking. She put these thoughts to one side and considered her next step while she dried her hair.

Should she tell Felix now or later or do some more research first? Or spend some time first Googling real estate in Aliante and checking Google Earth to see if she could find something that corresponded to Erin's description of the house, and then decide what to do next. She threw on a T-shirt and a pair of jeans and sat down at the little table to start her search.

It is quite easy to find, because the details supplied by Erin made it possible to be very specific. Miranda typed "Alicante, villa, 5 bedrooms, 3 car garage, tennis court, lap pool" into the search engine and only two places popped up, both on the website of a real estate firm that seemed to specialize in luxury properties. One with five bedrooms and one with five plus a study. She copied both addresses just in case and entered one at a time into Google Earth and studied them. The five-bedroom house without a study was definitely Erin's dream house, every detail fitted. She returned to the real estate website and looked at all the photos of the property and was amazed at the opulence. The house was very expensive and there was nothing to indicate that anyone was negotiating to buy it yet.

Chapter 14

Agonizing about how to tell Felix would have to wait, decided Miranda, as she drove to Thornhill. There was no way she could launch into this story when they were on their way out. It might ruin the evening and she mustn't let him see she was worried about how he would take this either. She knew without a doubt that it might be a make-or-break moment when she told him what she had done. He had already forgiven her for invading his privacy, researching the house fire and all about him personally, and surveilling him with hidden CCTV, but would he tolerate another incursion into his private life, and into that of his wife, however villainous she was?

She slowed when she turned into the long driveway up to the gates, bundled up her worry and pushed it into the far back of her mind. Rounding the last bend, she saw the gates wide open and smiled at the sight. How nice not to have to get out to open them, not that she was planning to drive in, but anyway. She stopped by the front steps and Felix came out, looking handsome in black jeans and a white shirt open at the neck. And sexy, she thought, long legs and a nice backside, but I can't think of that now.

'Come and see the garden,' he said as soon as she got out. 'Some of it looks quite lovely now – as do you, very lovely!'

She had only packed one good dress for the week, expecting all her social interactions to be very casual affairs, coffee in a café, drinks in a bar, maybe a pub lunch. But now she was absurdly pleased that she had packed her second prettiest dress, lime green with a pattern of tiny dark blue and white squares like little tiles scattered over it. She knew it was flattering and when she had put it on, she stood in front of the full-length mirror and wondered if Felix would think she looked attractive. She even bent closer to the glass to look into her own hazel eyes, always more green than brown when she wore this dress, to see them as he would. Silly girl! she said to herself at the time, you're too old for this, this is what teenagers do, put a lid on it!

They walked around the house to the formal garden that had been a riot of weeds last time she looked, and she stopped with an exclamation when they turned the corner.

'Good Lord! You must have been working all day — you've done the entire rose garden. It was a disaster zone a month ago, it must have been knee-high in weeds by now. Did you find what you needed in the stables?'

'I thought that locked door at the end might have been a tack room and probably where the garden equipment and the mower are kept, but I couldn't find a key — maybe that lawn mowing man has it? I pried the weeds out with a very large carving fork I found in the back of a drawer — the kind you use to hold the turkey down when you carve it, but I've cleaned it up. And it was easy to weed after the rain, just dirty.'

'You shouldn't have done so much, not without gloves and proper tools. Way beyond the call of duty!'

He held out his hands, 'I had to nearly scrub my skin off, but I found a nailbrush in one of the bathrooms — lucky find, or I would have had to use my toothbrush to get my nails clean.'

Half-way along the path to Amber and Torsten's front door Miranda slowed and said quietly, 'They're bound to ask you things and try to find out all kinds of personal details, so I'll beg your pardon in advance on their behalf. I've told everyone you are a friend from Bristol and the curiosity will be rampant. I've not had a male beside me around here since high school and tomorrow the gossip will be flying around like shrapnel.'

Felix laughed and stood back when Miranda rang the bell, and she was immediately proved right. People clustered around her as soon as they walked in and Felix waited and watched while she was hugged and kissed by nearly everyone present. She made the introduction as casual as she could, as if he was someone she'd known for a long time. 'This is my friend Felix from Bristol, and I won't bother to tell him your names, because he'll probably forget them in a minute.'

She took the bag with the wine and pate from Felix's hand and walked towards the kitchen to find Amber, and Felix stayed where he was. Amber was busy getting cutlery out, but she interrupted herself to subject Miranda to a medium-intensity interrogation starting with, 'I was just coming out – I saw someone opened the door, and I had a look to see who had arrived. Nice looking chap! How long have you known him? I never heard you say a word about him before! Is he local?'

Miranda knew from long experience that Amber would suspect something hidden and then try to dig it out if Miranda's answer was too brief, so she said, "Oh yes, I brought Felix. I've known him for ages in Bristol, but I've only just discovered that he's doing a locum job in Exeter, so I thought I'd bring him along. And he is *very* interested to meet you.'

'Why? What have you told him about me?'

Miranda laughed. 'Sorry, that came out all wrong! Felix is the guy who came to fill in for Torsten, so he knows everyone at the firm, and when I said I was coming here tonight and mentioned your name, he decided to come with me. I hope you don't mind!'

'God no! A nice-looking spare man is always good. You go out and get yourself a glass of something and I'll be with you in a moment.'

Miranda obeyed and found Felix in the living room talking to a group of five, looking completely relaxed and composed. She joined them just in time to hear Amber's younger sister Tilly, ask Felix how long he had known Miranda and wondered what he would say. 'Two days' or 'Just met her'? But no, he must have seen her approach out of the corner of his eye, reached out very casually and put his arm around her shoulders, pulled her close and said, 'Long enough.' Everybody laughed, and Tilly cast a sly look at Miranda and made a kissing face.

Much later, after dinner and quite a lot of wine, Lilian, wobbling slightly in her high heels, cornered Miranda and Felix and tried to pry details of their relationship out of them, concentrating on Felix. After a couple of minutes, he asked calmly, 'Do you think Rose described me well in that text message last night?'

Miranda burst out laughing and Lilian went beetroot red and stared at him, then she giggled. 'You're one of a kind, all right! Hold on to him, Mirrie – he's a keeper.'

As she tottered away, Miranda shook her head. 'Sorry! But I did warn you – and that bit about the text was perfect!'

When they were about to get into the car Felix said, 'There's no need to drive me back – just go back to your hotel and I'll take a taxi from there.'

And Miranda stopped with her hand on the driver's door, looked at him across the roof of the car and said firmly, 'Now listen, Felix! I've spent an entire evening drinking tonic with the same damn slice of lemon in it, apart from one glass of wine with dinner - especially so I can drive you home, so stop talking about taking a taxi. I wasn't going to risk it again, after all the wine we'd had at Thornhill when I drove back the other night and thankfully didn't get stopped. So please, don't waste my sacrifice!'

As they passed Shillingford St George she started to feel uncertain about what might develop. This wasn't like her at all, and it was such an unusual situation. She was taking him to her house where he was living, and then she was returning to the hotel. Who should say, 'do you want to/can I come in for a coffee?' What if she said it, and he took it as her wanting to get him into bed, which she did, of course, but if he didn't want that, would he decline? Or should she leave it to him? She had never been so conflicted about a man in her life. Maybe she was making too much of those little touches, and though she had initiated a couple, the way he had put his arm around her at Amber's and pulled her so close. Was that a public demonstration of belonging or possession, or a signal to her, or just a way of creating some gossip? And tomorrow she would have to tell him that she had found out where Erin was, and it might all go wrong, and their little beginnings would crumble.

Still uncertain, she stopped outside the gates, and Felix said calmly, 'I'll open the gates' and got out without waiting for an answer. He walked ahead up the drive and around the circular rose bed, and she drove slowly behind him and noticed that he had left the hall light on. She got out of the car, while Felix unlocked the door and stood to one side holding it open for her. Her heart began to beat very fast and though she'd had hardly had anything to drink, she felt slightly dizzy. He closed the door and turned her around to face him, and then they were in a tight clinch, and he kissed her as if he couldn't wait a moment longer.

Chapter 15

Miranda woke up at her usual time and yawned. Sleeping a bit longer would have been lovely after getting back to the hotel very late. Felix hadn't wanted her to go back, but to wake up in his bed and then tell him what she must tell him today had felt unthinkable. She must create a break in the timeline, a distance to separate last night from this morning, just in case it all went wrong.

She texted Felix after thinking carefully about how to phrase it, unsure of how much to say. No way was she going to take anything that happened in the night as a commitment by him, it might just have been that he fancied her and liked the sex, and she felt a need to reassure him that the house was his home for as long as he needed it, and she wouldn't come and go without warning.

May I call in at Thornhill this morning on my way to Bristol? M

His reply made her laugh with relief. *Are you daft? It's your house, Lady C, come any time you like, I'm just the gamekeeper. F*

But once she was there and they sat down with cups of coffee, this time in the smaller living room that got the most morning sun, she didn't know how to start. They sat in the tapestry-covered armchairs with wooden armrests, that her grandmother re-covered when Miranda was a little girl. Her grandparents had used this room all the time, for morning tea in the winter, sitting in these chairs with the little round marquetry table between them and a fire in the white fireplace, and to watch the news on TV or to entertain a visitor over a drink. She had never once felt uncomfortable in this room before, and somehow the contrast between the childhood memories and how she felt now made it harder to start.

Her bundled up worry parcel had come undone, and now it was right there in the room with them, making conversation awkward and stilted.

While he made the coffee, after a low-key friendly kiss on the lips when she arrived, she had only been able to think of one thing, that she was going to risk alienating him. She had known this since she located Erin, but suddenly it was a very real possibility, a present threat. Each step she had taken, each intrusion into his affairs had made it more likely that he would tell her to butt out, that it was none of her business. The fact that she felt nobody else would help him sort out his life if she didn't do it, had no validity here. That he had seemed OK with her snooping and finding things out, the last time she told him what she had done, didn't mean that somewhere ahead of her wasn't an invisible boundary. And she knew that once she crossed that boundary, anything could happen. The thought of not even being friends with him made her feel very insecure. And what did that kiss when she arrived mean, so without emotional emphasis. Was the sex last night just lust?

So now she told him about the four texts she had already had from people who were at the party, instead of talking about what she had found out. She made a funny story out of their curiosity, ranging from subtle hints to direct questions. He laughed and made some comments about what she told him, but his eyes were searching, and she felt more and more unnerved.

'There's something else going on,' said Felix and fixed her with that serious look of his. 'Something's happened since last night, hasn't it? You are worried. Is it about me? Are you concerned that I'll be hurt if you're not serious about what happened last night?'

He looked steadily at her while she hesitated very briefly about how to start. 'Yesterday I had an idea and

I … did some more research.' Here she petered out, frozen into silence by apprehension.

'Miranda, for God's sake - what is it? You have found something out, something bad, haven't you? Please, just tell me.'

'No, no – it's nothing bad! I'm just worried you'll be angry. I might have gone too far this time. I had a text conversation with Erin.'

She said the last bit very quickly and held her breath, but all he did was stare at her. 'You what? Texted Erin – how the hell did you know her phone number? It can't be her old number because I get a 'not available' response if I try. Not that I've tried for a while, but I did call and text when she first disappeared.'

'I got it off her Facebook page. Perhaps she just blocked your number, or maybe she's got a new phone? But she replied.'

'Why? She doesn't know you.' He didn't look angry, but that might mean nothing. His self-control was incredible, she knew this already.

'I pretended to be someone else.' She got up and walked over to the window and leaned against the deep windowsill, so she could face him from a distance. Starting at the very beginning she told him the whole story, every detail and answered his questions, and all the time she was intensely aware that he was not revealing what he was thinking or feeling. His eyes were on her face throughout, but his expression didn't change. And finally, when she reached the end, he got to his feet and came over to where she was standing. 'Can I see?'

Miranda pulled the phone out of her jeans pocket, opened the text folder and held it out. She felt a current of unease as real as a cold wind and turned around to looks out the window, while behind her Felix read the texts.

'Well!' he said after a couple of minutes and she swung around, unsure of what this single-word exclamation meant. Felix gripped her shoulders just like he had last night and pulled her towards him, his arms tightened around her, and she was so relieved that she let herself slump against his chest. 'Oh, Felix!' she said in a muffled voice against his shirt. 'I've been so scared.'

He let her go and look into her face. 'You were scared - of me? Why?'

She realised how that had sounded and smiled. 'Not of you! But of your reactions. And I have some ideas.'

'I would be very surprised, if you didn't have some ideas,' he said, and there was that smile that she was hoping for, the smile that turned him into the person she wanted to please more than anyone else she knew. 'Are you going to tell me?'

'I need another coffee. I've been so nervous all

morning I could hardly eat breakfast. In case I finally overstepped the line, and you'd tell me to butt out. I could hardly bear to start telling you.'

'There is no line,' he said simply. 'Not between you and me. So, let's make another coffee and you can tell me your ideas.'

And she remembered some of the things he said while they made love in the night, and her heart leapt in her chest, This was real, he wanted her, it was written all over his face, and she could hear it in his voice.

This time they sat at the kitchen table, and she thought how odd it was that she felt as if they had done this many times before, sat here across from each other talking over coffee, but it was only the second time.

'This is the idea, the main one,' said Miranda and got up to fish around in her bag for the biscuits she bought on the way, ripped the packet open and put it on the table between them. 'If you report it to the police along with all the evidence that we've found ...'

Felix held up his hand, 'Evidence that *you* have found.'

'Whatever! Doesn't matter, but if you do, or your lawyer does, then it would take years to get that money back, if it really went to the Caymans, and the legal feels would be horrific. And it could all go wrong, they might move the money again, it's a situation loaded with pitfalls. I checked and the Caymans is a haven for tax avoidance, tax evasion, hiding ill-gotten gains and forming shell companies that don't have to reveal *anything* about who owns them, so you can do nearly anything there. I thought the best thing would be to let them go ahead and buy that luxury mega-villa and then the cops can prosecute her, and the court will enforce a sale and you get the money back. Because I'm sure Erin wouldn't be able to claim her part, if there was a part that was hers – as she would have been able to before she stole it all, because I don't think you're allowed to profit from crime. Have a biscuit, before they get cold.'

Now he laughed with genuine amusement. 'That's so funny the way you say that about things that were never hot. I've never heard anyone do it before.'

'Granda said it a lot, it was one of our jokes.' She smiled at the memory that brought back countless occasions from her childhood.

They got Felix's laptop connected to the modem and Miranda showed him the real estate advertisement and all the photos of the house in Alicante.

'Jesus, the ostentation!' Felix went back through the pictures and studied the lavish interiors. 'And look at the furniture, fit for an Arab prince and hideous - not to mention the bathrooms and all those gold taps.'

'The furniture comes with the house, it's a package deal. Did you really get that much for your house, after the mortgage was paid back and all those things –

enough for them to pay for that palace? I presume you had a mortgage?'

'Do you have one?' he asked, and of course she didn't, and it made her embarrassed that she was so lucky, that everything had been handed to her on a plate and there was no need for her to worry about anything. Not that he knew about the money, but the house alone was an astounding thing to own at her age. And then it dawned on her that he was teasing and behind that serious expression sat a secret smile. It's lovely, she thought, how I'm beginning to read him quite well.

'No, I don't,' she said. 'I wouldn't think this house was ever mortgaged and I've done nothing to deserve to be so lucky, it's just fate and circumstance. I only asked because I wondered where so much money was coming from. I mean, enough for them to buy that extravagant villa.'

'Well, it could be that Ralph has hidden money too, though it seems unlikely. If I remember rightly, he was a sales manager for a plumbing company or something, so he can't have any huge secret savings hidden from his wife. Unless he won it, perhaps? He did gamble big on the horses, that was obvious when we went with that group to the races, where that photo was taken. His wife was rolling her eyes at the size of his bets.'

'It's got to have come from somewhere, not just earnings, whether it was horse race winnings or a lottery win,' said Miranda and picked up another biscuit. 'And if they haven't got enough money to buy that outrageous house without a mortgage, could they get a mortgage in Spain? Don't you have to prove that you're able to pay the interest, that you have a job? I thought that was what you have to do when you borrow money from the bank. Prove you are earning money, not just have some saved up?'

'You do, yes – and may I say that I'm quite relieved to find there's something you haven't researched? I'm not being mean, but you're such an outstanding chaser down of facts, a legendary researcher.'

'I love research, I really do. I should have stayed on and done my masters instead of going to New Zealand for that job when I graduated. I would have had my master's degree now and I might even have a job in a field I'm interested in, instead of one that rather bores me.'

'Was it true then? I thought you said you lied to the man you talked to at Avon Fire,' says Felix.

Miranda thought back to what she might have said. 'Oh, I see! Sorry! I didn't mean to mislead you, I meant I lied about being a journalist, the rest was true. I've got a BEng from Bristol.'

'Aha!' said Felix. 'I thought that lie was going a bit far, but it was true! What kind of engineering?'

'All my final year optional papers were on specialist structural topics, anything that involved complex calculations of weight and balance, and steel and concrete, you could say.'

'And what do you like best? What kind of topic would you pick for a master's thesis, if you could choose anything at all?'

Slightly surprised Miranda realised that he was really interested, and for the first time, she saw the connection between her studies and his profession. Of course, he was interested, because they knew a lot of the same things, and how strange it was that she had not thought of it before.

Aloud she said, 'The thing I like more than anything is a very specialized area that fits perfectly with what I had chosen to study in my last year. Something I discovered I loved working with when I was in New Zealand. There they build a lot of quite way-out houses in tricky places. I was lucky enough to be involved in the specifications for two cantilevered buildings, that's what I like best. It doesn't matter if it's a house or a hotel or the café at the top of a gondola – anything jutting out from rock faces, from steep hill slopes, cliffs – anything! The challenges involved are similar – working out the combination of the site contours, the geology, the water table, runoff versus drainage, how to anchor things, counterweight and balance. It's like a whole little specialized world of facts that you have to work through and get exactly right.'

He sat there on the other side of the kitchen table

and just looked at her without comment, and just as she was beginning to think that last statement was a bit childishly over-enthusiastic, he reached across and took the uneaten biscuit out of her hand. 'Lick your fingers, you amazing girl – you've got melted chocolate chips spreading like a fungus. How old are you?'

'Nearly twenty-nine – in June.' She knew he would be as a least ten years older and waited to see where this was going to lead, but surprisingly, he didn't follow up on this statement, and she excused herself to go to the toilet.

When she returned, he reverted to what they were talking about before he asked her age. 'But to carry on where we left off – Erin and I had a small mortgage, very small for such an expensive house. I owned a house when we met, I'd bought it when prices were a lot lower, about ten years earlier and I sold it at an indecent profit. But I discovered something, and only by chance really, when I was dealing with the bank, trying to find out where all the insurance money had gone. First, she transferred it to another bank in this country, and into the same account she had also transferred money from a third account held by a different bank again. I couldn't understand it at first, where had she got it from? The bank she had transferred our money to – the first step – they cooperated when approached by my bank, told me some basic facts and mentioned that second large amount. And then I checked our joint account, went back and scrutinized the patterns of debits and credits, thinking she might have syphoned off money regularly for ages, knowing I never checked the account. And I discovered that her sales commissions had ceased coming into our joint account over a year earlier, and we had in effect lived and paid for everything out of my earnings, while she had salted hers away for her big escape. And she earned a lot!'

'What a bitch!' says Miranda. 'And she knew you trusted her and that you never looked at the details of the account. She deserves to be whipped! I hope you'll divorce her quick smart!'

'We aren't married, we never got around to it. I bought the house three and a half years ago when we got together – Erin's firm had it for sale, and I bought it because I like Clifton. If I said I'd been thinking of a separation, I didn't mean like when you're married. I mean to split, to go our separate ways. And I should never have had a joint account with her anyway – that just started as a kind of house expenses account, and then we decided we might as well use it like a proper joint account. I took everything on trust.'

'How *could* you be so slack! I can't believe it!' Miranda was outraged at the thought of Felix not being more careful. 'It's unbelievable! You need someone you can trust to look after you and your affairs, you daft man!'

And he said casually and without any drama, 'Maybe you could?'

There was total silence for a long moment, the only sound was the quiet humming of the fridge. She couldn't look at him, she was overwhelmed, as if her heart was holding its breath.

Then Felix said, 'Please don't feel you have to reply! It just popped out before I could clamp my teeth together. We'll just forget I said it.'

'No!' she exclaimed and leapt to her feet, for some reason she didn't understand. 'No, we will *not*! I refuse to forget it! You said it and it stands. Yes, I will. I can't think of anything in the world I would rather do. Isn't it odd, I've only known you for five minutes, and I feel as if I've known you all my life.'

She pointed up at the camera in the corner and her eyes, serious now, met his. 'I looked at you for half an hour the other night before I came here to confront you. And I went back and studied you over and over, and I thought, that's a totally gorgeous man. And it wasn't just that you're good looking, it was something about you. Your tidiness and the way you move, just like a ... No, I won't say it, such a cliché. And I love how self-possessed and calm you are. And when you sat down to read you sat perfectly still, relaxed and didn't fidget. You're so special! And I knew you weren't dangerous, so I wasn't scared to come here – I was just careful in case I upset you. I felt I knew you already.'

Now Felix was on his feet too and they stood an arm's length apart, looking at each other without moving, until he said, 'You've still got some chocolate on your left forefinger,' and they both started laughing.

'Come here,' he said, and she took two steps into his embrace.

Part II

JUNE

They were sitting on the terrace on a sunny June morning, cool with a promise of heat later in the day. Felix looked out over the garden and said, 'You know, I really enjoy this. Look at the roses! I read up on roses yes, I can see the smile, I know I told you I'm not a gardener. But I'm enjoying it, And to get back to the point, I've read all about deadheading and summer pruning and winter pruning – it's a little bubble of science that I never knew existed. I've got it all stored away to apply as the season rolls on. In short, I'm an instant expert. And you must come and look at the delphiniums, they've just opened up.'

'Felix,' said Miranda, her forehead creased with concern. 'Are you feeling OK? Delphiniums? Two months ago, you couldn't tell a sunflower from a hawthorn hedge and now you're talking about delphiniums – I can't believe it.'

He shook his head and grinned at her disbelief. 'I know, it's crazy, but since I took on the weeding I've fallen in love with the garden, and because I have no idea what the plants are called, I use that app – you know, you take a picture of a plant or a tree and the app finds the name and lots of other photos of the same thing so you can check it really is the right one. And it kind of continues from there, next you're clicking on a link to another page with more information and before you know it, an hour has passed. It is very comforting and calming to do something that pleases a plant – no demands, no urgency and you feel good when you've done it.'

The early June sunshine reflected off the windows behind them and created an illusion of light coming from all directions. Miranda had arrived from Bristol the previous evening in time for a late supper and today promised to be perfect for being outside.

She looked at him and couldn't help smiling; tanned and with his hair ruffled as it always seemed to be, completely relaxed and the change in him seemed unreal. Just two months and this was the result of peace and calm and a normal, happy life. And there was no doubt that he was happy and that he loved the place already. But it was hard to believe that he actually enjoyed doing the weeding. Miranda could think of few things that were more tedious and would rather be pruning trees. She laughed inside at the thought that this was the same man who told her he had hired someone to come in and remove everything that needed more maintenance than mowing, when he bought a new house, and who only had shrubs and trees and grass? And now he walked around the garden every morning and checked how the plants were doing and probably talked to them too, when she wasn't there to hear it.

She voiced this thought, and Felix looked thoughtful for a moment and said, 'This place has got under my skin. I've never felt like this about a house before. It's the architecture and the garden in combination, it is a re-created period piece. Your great-great -whatever he was, he had a feeling for proportion, and for creating visual interest. Look at the way you come out of the French doors behind us, across this terrace and onto the lawn, and the roses form a semi-circular boundary with that dark little hedge behind them.'

Miranda followed his pointing finger and listened quietly. 'And then you walk down the path through the gap in the centre of the curved hedge and suddenly you're in a cottage garden full of herbaceous flower beds, all the colours under the sun all mixed up, and the meadow beyond that with the fruit trees. I mean, who could resist becoming interested? Not to mention that old glasshouse, Did they grow vegetables?'

'According to that book with all the details about Thornhill I showed you in the study, they grew all their own vegetables in the era when it was built, but my grandparents only used the glasshouse for propagating seedlings and cuttings. It hasn't been used properly for a couple of generations I wouldn't think. Oh, wait – during the second world war they went back to growing vegetables, and they had chickens in half of it. You know how there's a wooden structure about halfway down the length of it with wire netting? The hens' half was behind that.'

'When are you putting it on the market? Should we tidy up the glasshouse first?'

Miranda stared at him without any idea what he was talking about. Was he expecting her to sell this place and move with him somewhere else? Was it possible that they had totally misunderstood each other?

'Sell it? Don't you *want* to live here? I thought you said you could work from anywhere and travel to see clients.' Her voice was shocked, nearly frantic.

Felix sat up straighter and stared at her. 'But I thought that was your plan! When you came here that first evening, you said something like, "I'm not going to live here, you can stay for a while" and I've assumed you were planning to sell it and invest the money, use it for other things. Of course, I'd love to live here, but can you afford to keep it?'

Miranda let out the breath she hadn't realised she was holding, smiled in relief and felt her clenched insides relax. She reached across the little table and took his hand. 'I *don't* want to sell it. I never thought of it after the first few days. It's a family place, full of history and tradition, even though it's not a mansion or a castlc. I mean, it's five generations who have lived here. I love this place! When I handed in my notice, that's what I thought we would do, live and work from here, you work from here and I get a job in Exeter.'

'Wow!' said Felix, a word she had never heard him use before, so very un-Felix that it made her laugh. 'To be allowed to go on living and working here – that's amazing. I'll have to get used to the idea, it's a bit overwhelming.'

Miranda suddenly wondered what else they hadn't discussed in detail, what else did they had different assumptions about, or what he didn't know. The last two months had been a hiatus a bit like a fragmented honeymoon, with her coming over from Bristol in the weekends, and somehow their time together seemed to have mostly involved sex, eating nice food, drinking wine and endlessly talking, but not in any detail about the future.

'Listen Felix,' she said now, 'we've got to get serious! All this rampant sex and drinking too much wine and sitting on the terrace drinking coffee. Not to mention eating far too many chocolate chip biscuits. It's great fun, I love it! But I'm suddenly worried that we aren't on the same page in the book of life – sorry, what a cliché! So maybe we should fact-check our impressions of what you think I want, and what I think you want?'

'I don't really want anything in particular, apart from you,' said Felix. 'I've become a drifter. I have few possessions, I can work anywhere, and as I heard my dad tell you when we went to see him, it's like I might become a tramp with a profession.'

'OK, let me ask you a few simple questions. Number one: do you absolutely and totally want to live here and work from here, or maybe from an office in Exeter?'

He wasn't sure if she was serious, she could see it in the assessing look he gave her. 'I'm serious, darling. I was never more serious, so tell me honestly,' she said to prompt him to reply.

'Of course, I want us to live in this house and work from here, I can think of nothing better.'

'Good,' said Miranda in a businesslike way. 'Number two: do you want to look after the garden forever or should I get a gardener in, maybe fortnightly. It's a big job and it might take up too much of your time. There's no way I want to do it after spending years being Gramma's garden slave - that was enough for a lifetime.'

'Oh, for goodness' sake, don't hire a gardener! I like it and maybe you'll give me a hand now and then. Keep the lawn mowing guy on, though. It takes him two hours on the ride-on to mow it all and then he does the edges and cleans the mower. But the crucial thing is, can we afford it between us? Now that I've got my computer and my software, and everything is up and running again, I'll be working like I used to and earning money, which is fine in a normal kind of setting. But this place is expensive, the annual costs must be huge.'

And Miranda clapped a palm on her forehead. 'God, Felix! I don't think I ever told you, sorry! I inherited a lot of money too, about half a million. Which earns interest.'

He looked without focus into space for so long she couldn't imagine what his expressionless face was hiding and was just about to ask, when he finally spoke.

'In that case there are a couple of things we must do. The most pressing one is a contract, either between us as living-together partners or if you agree to marry me, a pre-nuptial agreement. You've got to have all this wealth safe-guarded whatever we do.'

'What do you mean, if I want to marry you? Of course, I want to marry you, you daft man!'

He got up and pulled her to her feet and held her close. 'I'm glad I never knew about all that money before today. This property was bad enough. At least you know I love you for yourself, not for your incredible inheritance.'

'Oh, good,' said Miranda and smiled up into his face, her hazel eyes twinkling. 'But isn't it great that we *can* keep Thornhill because it costs quite a bit every year. The interest on the invested money will pay for the upkeep of Thornhill without touching the capital unless the house needs a new roof or something drastic. But I warn you now. I don't think I have it in me to be an out-and-out capitalist, so to ease my conscience about all this unearned wealth I'll support some charities in a substantial way once I have a new job and earn real money again. I'll tell you the details later of what the expenses for this property are – I'm sure most people don't realise.'

'You researched it and worked it out, I presume, like you do everything, you thorough girl?'

'Of course - I've got a spreadsheet with all the figures if you want to see it. I'm leaving the money in Government bonds for now, it seems a safe thing to do, and the return is goodish. And I've got another income source that you don't know about. I can't tell you, I'll have to show you, but not right now.'

Over the last couple of months, she had progressively moved more things from her flat in Bristol to Thornhill. Clothes and personal belongings, and some boxes that had been sitting unopened in a corner of the front hall.

'Let's go for a walk in the garden,' said Felix and surprised her once again with how he can wait for things, instead of saying 'oh, please, show me now' like most people would in this situation. Instead, he said, 'let's go for a walk'.

'I *do* love you, Felix! I can't wait for us to live together properly. If that stupid job hadn't had the clause about not resigning during a project, I'd be living here right now.'

'Very unusual.' Felix walked ahead down the three steps to the lawn. 'I'd never heard of anything like it before. What exactly does it say?'

'That key personnel cannot leave before completion of any major project where they hold key knowledge of the development process and the decisions it is based on. Or you face a penalty. And I don't want to abandon the project anyway – it's been moderately interesting, and I want to see it through. It should be all over by the middle of July. I've told the landlord I'm giving up the flat at the end of July, to be on the safe side. Gives me time to sort things out.'

'And what is the potential penalty?'

'They tie you to a post and pelt you with rotten eggs and leave you in the sun for the rest of the day. No wait! That's not it, sorry, that's something else. You forfeit your project bonus, and it's quite a substantial bonus and I'd like to have it.'

They were tidying up after lunch when Felix remembered Miranda's promise. 'What is this second income stream? I've been trying to guess, but I can't. Is it internet based?'

'Nope – it's in a couple of those boxes I left in the hall. You stay here and I'll get them, and I'll unpack them on the kitchen table.' She did two trips while he loaded the dishwasher, put the boxes on the table and pointed at a chair. 'You can sit there and watch.'

Out of the first box came packets of toothpicks and wooden skewers, glue tubes, little boxes of mysterious powders and lumps of something that looked like grubby white plasticine. Miranda lined everything up in a tidy row and lifted a thick towel out of the bottom of the box. Felix watched in silence, knowing he was being kept in deliberate suspense, and waited for the second box to be unpacked. She slid him an amused glance and opened the next carton and lifted out a shoe box, then another shoe box and two wobbly stacks of small pottery bowls and last a couple of plates.

'Right! This is my little sideline, or hobby, I suppose you could call it. Kintsugi – based on the ancient Japanese philosophy called wabi-sabi, which is about seeing the beauty in broken or imperfect objects.'

She opened one of the shoe boxes, unwrapped a cloth and revealed five pieces of broken pottery, with glaze streaked with black and grey. 'This is the next one I'm going to work on, and here is one I did the other day.'

She lifted a small bowl, dark brown with a ribbed effect, out of the box and handed it to Felix, who turned it his hands, fascinated. 'It's beautiful, like a work of art it *is* a work of art! So, you break them and then you mend them with this glue that looks like gold? How lovely – and how clever.'

'It's fun,' said Miranda and took another mended bowl out of the box. 'You never know quite how it will look until it's all pieced together. There are lots of different ways of doing it and you can use real powdered gold or a gold substitute. I nearly always use the substitute. You can do it by mixing the epoxy glue with the gold and applying it, quite sparingly, so the gold veins come out slightly different widths depending on how much glue is squeezed out of the join, and it takes time. Or alternatively, you can glue the joins and then apply a thick filler and dust the gold powder over before the filler dries. That way you have much more control over the veins, how wide they are and if there are chips of glaze missing you fill them. It's much slower this way, but the result is better. But whichever way you do it, you can only attach one piece at a time and then you have to hold it in place for a few minutes until the glue dries a bit and then you can do another piece, if you don't put too much pressure on it.'

'Very fiddly and precise work and you'd need a lot of patience. What if a shard has ragged edges, or bits missing from the glaze when you break the bowl?'

'Then I just fill the little spaces where fragments are missing, with the glue mixed with the gold mica powder. There is a technique for filling in where a big piece is missing, but it's very tricky. The hardest part is learning how to break them nicely – it took me ages. You want at least three pieces, but if you get a lot of small ones, it gets messy. And preferably not too many chips of glaze missing. A bowl can take a couple of hours if it's in many pieces. And then it must sit and cure for a couple of days. The epoxy glue I use holds after five minutes, but it's not fully cured.'

Felix was looking at the row of bowls veined with gold joints that she has lined up while they talked; eight beautiful objects created with care and patience. 'You are the most surprising girl! One surprise after another. Who buys them?'

'Oh, all kinds of people. I have them on a website and in a gallery in Bristol – they sell lots of them. And occasionally I get asked to do a precious bowl or plate that someone broke and when they get it back, I sometimes get a message or a call, and they say, it's more precious than it was before. Isn't that lovely?'

'Show me how you break one.'

She picks up one of the bowls she bought in the Exeter second-hand shop, holds it so it's resting on its side and breaks it with a sharp blow using the side of her fist. 'See, it's the angle and sharpness of the blow that makes it work, I think.'

'I wondered what the towel was for – but now I can see why you have it. Very, very clever! Can I break one, please?'

'Of course, and don't worry if it ends up crushed - none of these were expensive. I'm constantly trawling through second-hand shop to find the right type and size of bowl, sometimes plates, but I prefer bowls.'

He chops down hard and the bowl breaks nicely into four clean-edged pieces. 'Wow! You're an instant expert, you can do some more if you like. I have some zip-lock bags here that we can put the pieces in, so they don't get mixed up.'

While Felix satisfied his urge to break things, she went upstairs to the bedroom, that used to be her grandparents' room, which they now shared. That first weekend when she came down, after that intense day when she confessed that she had found and texted Erin, they moved furniture around all over the top floor, until they had the large bedroom just the way they wanted it. Kids in a toy store, she thought while she unpacked her little weekend bag, but the room looks terrific now.

Amber called as she was walking towards the stairs, and Miranda stopped and gazed out at the meadows from the window on the landing while they talked.

'I know it's short warning, but would you two like to come for dinner? Tonight? It's Tilly's birthday and Torsten said he wants to get to know Felix better and thank him for covering for him while he was away. And as an added attraction we have Harold with us this weekend, or with Tilly. He came down on the bus and I thought you might give him a lift back tomorrow, if you can stand the thought of being cooped up with him?'

'We'd love to! What time and what can I bring.'

'Nothing, truly nothing! Just bring that lovely hunk of yours and remember to say Happy Birthday to Tilly!'

At half past six Amber opened the door and exclaimed, 'Jeez Louise! You didn't really bring all that for Tilly, did you?'

'Of course, we did,' said Felix and kissed her cheek. 'But she'll have to share the wine with the rest of us.'

'Tilly, Happy Birthday! And don't you look lovely – what a pretty hairstyle.' Miranda hugged Tilly and then stood back to look at her properly. 'I don't think I've ever seen you with your hair off your forehead before, it suits you, very elegant.'

Torsten appeared from the garden, wearing a barbecue apron, and Felix handed Tilly the things he was still holding. 'Roses from the Thornhill garden, a bottle of something Miranda claims is better than good, and a special gift from Miranda.'

'Thank you both!' Tilly was blushing and excited looking. She piled everything into Harold's arms and held her arm up high and wiggled her fingers. 'We got engaged!'

It wasn't until they had drinks in their hands and were standing around the barbecue that Tilly opened the little parcel. She held the tiny bowl up and said, 'Oh my God - that is so beautiful! Where did you get it?' She turned it round and round in her hands, looking at the veins of gold. 'It's been broken and put together again – I know what this is, it's Japanese, isn't it? I saw pictures a while ago, but I can't remember what it's called.'

'Kintsugi,' said Felix, 'and Miranda made it.' And Miranda was pelted with questions and repeated the explanation in an abbreviated form, explained what the kintsugi tradition means, and what she did with them.

'Wabi-sabi – what a fabulous word,' said Harold, who had said nothing since they arrived. 'Beauty in flawed objects, I love it. Like what Tilly sees in me.' He smiled at Tilly and she glowed with happiness.

Everyone watched them for a moment and Miranda thought what a nice guy he was, and that she wouldn't mind driving to Bristol with him in the car. Later, when the others started talking about gardens, she turned to him and offered him a ride back to Bristol with her the next day.

'Lovely, thank you,' he said. 'It's such drag on the bus, it takes twice as long as it does in a car – about three hours, but my car passed away after a short illness last month and I must get some more jobs before I can replace it.'

'What do you do?' asked Miranda and realised that so far nobody had told her anything about him, apart from the fact that Tilly met him at a party in someone's cottage near Salcombe and the few things that came up the first time she and Felix met him.

'I'm an actor. I've just been murdered in a new crime series for Netflix and now I'm out of work again. But you'll be able to see me lying at the base of a high voltage power pylon with my head smashed to bits early next year, such a colourful exit.' He laughed. 'It was a good part though, nearly six weeks in one stretch, which is great compared to some jobs - and I survived seven out of eight episodes.'

Inside Miranda's head neuron connections were popping like sparklers, this was perfect! But could she trust him? She managed to get another opportunity to talk to him one-to-one during the evening and thought that by the time they were halfway to Bristol, she might have given him a job.

Chapter 18

Sunday mornings had developed into a new routine since they spent the weekends together at Thornhill. They got up later and had breakfast on the terrace when the weather was warm enough, and today was no different.

'My God!' exclaimed Miranda suddenly in a guilty tone of voice. 'Oh, Felix, I've only just realised – I haven't cleaned this place once! Are you doing the housework during the week?'

'Of course. Wasting time on cleaning when we only have two days a week together would be silly, don't you think? And now that I'm working from here, I can do things when it suits me. But I'm not doing the rooms we don't use, just most of downstairs and our bedroom and bathroom.'

Miranda got up and walked around to hug him

from behind. 'I can't believe I never thought of it, I'm so sorry! I'm clearly not cut out to be a good housewife. It's just as well I have a career.'

When she picked up their cups and plates to take them to the kitchen, Felix suggested that they should go and and have a look at the glasshouse instead, and Miranda gradually understood that the conversation they had yesterday, about his mistaken belief that she was ultimately planning to sell Thornhill, had released him from holding back on ideas about what they could do.

'It's such a wonderful place,' he said as they walked around the long unused brick stables behind the house. 'And it has the potential to be so much more than it is – no criticism intended - but think of the resources available. If you don't want Thornhill to remain like a totally private oasis, we could run multiple lives here.' He slanted one of his not-quite-a-smile looks at her and opened the gate to the back field.

'Multiple lives? Now, that's a new one, please explain.'

Felix closed the gate behind them. 'Funny how I closed that just now. There's no livestock here and no dogs, but my natural instinct is to close gates. Never mind, I'll tell you what I mean.'

He leaned back against the gate and looked across the field towards the glasshouse. 'If we're going to live here, as I now know we are, then we have many choices of *how* we live here. Say for example that we decided to run a really top-notch B&B, which we could easily do. and it's one of those things you can turn on and off, so to speak. We could decide when to accept guests and when not to. So that's one life stream, if you like. And we could fix the glasshouse and reinstall the hen's half and have hens and sell or give away eggs. In the other half we could easily grow vegetables all year round. I've been reading about vegetables – not that I ever planted a single seed, but it seems that we could have two annual crops of some things.'

'You don't plant seeds, you sow them.' Miranda squinted against the sun glinting off the glasshouse and said slowly, thinking as she spoke. 'You're right – and a manor house kind of B&B with the added attraction of the hens and the vegetables and maybe a couple of lambs in the far field. Who knows? It could be a really nice thing to do. Gramma always referred to the field next to this one as the flower meadow. You can see the flowers even though the grass is quite tall. She scattered seeds in the spring to add to what was already there – Marguerite daisies, cornflowers, poppies and all kinds of wildflowers. The meadow would be mowed first, but not right down like a lawn, and the seeds from last year's flowers and the ones she scattered would germinate and the cycle would start again. The grass wasn't mowed this spring, so it doesn't look as it should, but it would be easy to get it right again next year.'

'But, and it's big but.' Felix turned to look at her. 'Do you want to take on a lot of different activities, that would involve people coming and going, a lot of extra work and maybe hiring someone part time. Or would you prefer another of my multiple life stream ideas? Because we could form a partnership, call ourselves something clever and trendy, and work together from here. It seems a shame to waste such a perfect combination – architecture and your kind of structural engineering. Or I could work from here and you could set yourself up as a separate business and become a consultant structural engineer for whoever needs to hire one, including me sometimes?'

They walked around the field and through the glasshouse and continued talking about the choices Felix had lined up. 'No need to make our minds up yet,' said Miranda and silently added inside her head, "let's wait and see how my venture pans out". Aloud she said, 'But I would love to work with you, and why would we rent an office and commute, when we can live and work in the same place?'

They returned to the house and Miranda took Felix straight to the formal sitting room, which she had been going to discuss with him ever since they started this living together in the weekends.

'This room is horrid – I've never liked it,' she said and turned in a circle to look around. 'We always sat in the smaller sitting room, where the TV is, and this one never felt comfortable to me when I was a child, and it still doesn't. It's like a remnant of the era when the house was built, when people had formal parties with lots of guests, it's not a comfortable feeling room. I don't know what's wrong with it. Gramma didn't like it either.'

Felix walked around and looked at the room from different angles, studied the furniture and returned to Miranda, who was still standing just inside the double doors watching him.

'The proportions are completely wrong,' he said decisively. 'You know about the so-called Golden Ratio – represented by the Greek letter phi? Or you can call it the "sixty-to-thirty-to ten" rule, which is the proportions between length, width and height. This room is very long for its width, and because the ceiling is so high it becomes spatially confusing. To me it looks as if it's nearly been tipped on its side. Not that it would make it perfect, but better than it is now.'

Miranda tried to image the room lying on its side and after a few moments she nodded and walked to one end of the long room, which had five tall windows down one side and the double doors on the opposite wall, and a huge columned fireplace at the far end.

'Of course! If what is now the height became the width, it would be much better. But there's nothing much we can do about that, is there?' Felix had a crease between his eyebrows and didn't respond, so she waited patiently. By now she knew that expression well; he was thinking and planning, visualizing something that didn't yet exist, and it was better not to disturb him, or he might lose the thread of his thinking.

Finally, his focus was back in the present moment, and he said, 'I think we could do something really nice with this room, very different from this formal and rather stilted space. Turn it into two spaces – not with a dividing wall, just the way it's arranged. And take out the middle window and put in double French doors that mimic the windows perfectly, so instead of looking out at the lawn, you could actually walk out onto a little terrace, which we would have to create, and go onto the lawn and walk across the grass to the look out over the flower meadow. Or maybe just three very wide steps like at the front door instead of a terrace.'

They spent the rest of the day moving furniture around until it was suddenly time for Miranda to pack her bag and pick up Harold. And now she sat outside Tilly's flat and watched with disbelief the number of times Harold turned back to give Tilly yet another hug, and how she then followed him to the car, and they kissed and hugged, until he finally got into the car and Miranda drove away quickly before they could start all over again.

Chapter 19

By the time they passed Beare, Miranda knew that Harold was perfect for the job she needed him to do, and she said quite casually, 'Harold, can I hire you to do an acting job for me?' He laughed and thought she was joking and she could tell he was waiting for the punchline, but she looked across at him and he realised she was serious. 'You're not kidding? What kind of job?'

'There's quite a back-story to this, Harold, so bear with me. If you understand what has happened already, you'll see that what I want to do isn't totally mad, it's doable – or so I hope. But this must stay strictly between you and me, *nobody* else must find out, or I might end up in terrible trouble. And I mean *terrible*! As in trouble with the law or worse, trouble with Felix. The potential for trouble is on the scale of seventy-five out of a hundred. On the other hand, if it comes off, Felix's life will be totally changed, and he will feel a lot better about things.'

Particularly about the disparity between what I have and what he no longer has, thought Miranda, but this was not something she was about to mention to Harold just now. She glanced across at him and their eyes met, and his expression was that of a child who has been given a mystery box with a promise of more to come.

'I can't wait to hear what it is! And you *can* rely on me. I'm very good at keeping secrets. I was always the one at school that the girls would tell their problems to, even very personal ones. As an example, I can tell you that two weeks ago I found out something about Amber, by accident, and she swore me to silence. I haven't said a single word about it even to Tilly.'

'Oh no, what is it?'

'I can't tell you, can I?'

They both laughed and Miranda could guess, but what mattered now was to tell Harold what had happened to Felix, and what she had found out since. Having considered how much to tell him before she even picked him up, she started with the arson suspicion, and why the fire service didn't suspect anything. From there to how consequently the insurance was paid out, that Erin stole all the money, and the effect it had on Felix's life and how it nearly broke him. She outlined her reasons for feeling certain it was arson and told him about the woman across the street, who saw the van being loaded. But she said nothing about Felix squatting at Thornhill or that she didn't already know him before all this happened. Aware of how nearly every single friend she had would react if she told them the truth of how she met Felix, she had not mentioned it to anyone. The short time she had known him before she decided she never wanted to let him go, the way she felt she trusted him even before she confronted him that evening at Thornhill, those are things she suspected nobody would understand. In fact, she wasn't sure she understood it herself.

Harold asked one question after another, all relevant and clever, and as she replied and explained she realised that Harold was the perfect partner in her plan, for many reasons aside from his acting ability. Not only did he ask about facts, he then extrapolated her assumptions and introduced new ideas about how Erin got away with it, and his grasp of the complicated story and all its details impressed her. When she had finished the story he said, 'Well, let's say that until now Erin got away with it, but I'm quite certain we can change that.'

'You're the perfect partner in crime.' Miranda laughed and glanced sideways at him. 'I thought you'd be great for this because of your acting experience, but you're so analytical and clever. This partnership was meant to be.'

When she stopped outside his flat, he paused with his hand on the door handle instead of getting out. 'The more I think of it, the angrier I feel on his behalf - for such a nice guy, such a trusting guy, to be gamed by that bitch - it's bloody awful. I think your plan is good. Let's do it and if it works it will change his life, as you said. But we need to discuss some parts of it a bit more, I think. It feels to me as if some of the detail is missing, and maybe there needs to be a kind of plan B in case of some hiccup that we haven't anticipated. I mean an alternative plan, like a whole separate strategy. It's no good trying to make ad hoc decisions if it turns ugly or something goes wrong. You've got to be at work this week, but I have loads of time, so I can get some of the stuff prepared, but we need to talk about it first. What are you doing tonight?'

She was so pleased with him she could have hugged him. 'I'm not doing anything in particular. Maybe we could continue planning over a pub dinner.'

Half an hour later they were sitting in a quiet corner of Harold's local, with large helpings of fish and chips in front of them and the notepad from Miranda's laptop bag beside her plate. Harold was clearly the type of man who thought well ahead and liked to make sure there would be no sloppy thinking or chance-taking in this venture.

'So where is that money going to go when we get it?' he asked and reached for the tomato sauce bottle. 'I mean, into which account? And we're going to need not only the account number but that code you need for transferring funds to another country – have you got that set up already?'

'It's going into Felix's account – not the one he had before, a new one. I suggested he should move to another bank, after how slack his original bank was. I mean, that they let Erin transfer all that money without notifying him defies belief, even if the account was shared. But as you said, he's far too trusting, or he was, probably not so much now! I still can't believe the cruelty of that woman, how she can live with herself after taking everything and leaving him destitute. But she did, and she deserves no mercy.'

She ate a few chips with her fingers and considered what came next. 'About eighty percent of the sum the insurance company paid out was Felix's share of the house, the money he put in when he bought it, and what was in that bank account was the net amount after the bank took the mortgage money back, but it was still a lot of money! So, when I pointed out that his old bank was perhaps not his best friend, he went to another bank and moved his personal stuff over. And this weekend I managed to sneak a look at the bank statement they emailed him at the end of May. I made a note of the new account number and I've got those international codes we need. And now I think of it, I must ask what his middle initial stands for, it's an A - I suspect it might be Alexander.'

'Why? It could be Alan or something.'

'I think his parents had an X fixation. His name is Felix Huxford – imagine a name with three x's!'

'Extraordinarily excessive,' said Harold without missing a beat. 'And what do you want me to start with this week? Don't you think they make great fish and chips here? The chips are always crisp, they never fail me – I can't bear soggy chips.'

'If you can organize the business cards, that would be great, seeing you've got all this spare time. My card must fit with the image I want to present,' said Miranda and picked up another chip and waved it at him. 'I want it to be very low-key and minimal and kind of confidence inspiring, no bright colours. I can't have my real cell phone number on it, Erin's seen that, so I'll buy a throw-away phone. I won't have a land line number on my card, but I might invent a London address. I've been thinking of a title, but it's a bit of a problem. I can't have anything that means I'm impersonating a lawyer - it's got to be something that can be taken as legal without actually saying it is. So, if you can come up with something suitable that I can be without actually saying I'm a lawyer, that would be great.'

After another bite of fish and a couple of chips, she smiled. 'You're right, these are perfect. We'll have to come here again. I think your card might be harder to design and I haven't thought as much about it, but we need a name for the firm you work for, something that sounds authoritative and a bit intimidating preferably. And I'll buy the air tickets online tonight, for Monday next week, back on Friday. And ...'

Harold nodded at someone behind Miranda and a voice said, 'How about an introduction to the lovely lady, Harry?' A slightly overweight man with a glass in his hand appeared beside Miranda's chair.

Harold replied without hesitating, 'Miranda, meet Jonathan, he's married to a lovely girl called Wendy. Jonathan, this is Miranda, my second cousin, married to Felix.'

'OK, I get it – nice to meet you, Miranda.' And Jonathan left with a swagger that bordered on a stumble.

'Pay no attention – he's nearly always borderline drunk, and incurably unfaithful. And sorry I turned you into a married cousin, but it seemed like a nice touch. Now where was I – yes, plan B or plans B in the plural. Say the guy gets violent. Do we leave or stay and fight it out? What do we use as a threat? And what if they're away for a few days and we miss them? We must plan how to stop them finding out where we're staying, so we don't end up with a scene in a hotel or a B&B. And are we leaving the business cards, or do we pick them up when we leave? And we've got to have some legal looking papers for them to sign, don't you think? To reinforce how heavily legal and binding everything is and that there's going to be evidence stored somewhere.'

'Jeez Louise, as Amber always says – you've done a lot of fast thinking! I have a little mental list of things to work out this week, you've mentioned a few of them. I think the cards must look very professional to give us credibility. So how about we kind of put them in front of Erin and Ralph as proof that we are the professionals we claim to be, and then we take them when we go and there is nothing left for them to show that anyone was there, so they can't prove they were coerced. Same with the papers, I'm going to create some kind of documents that looks seriously legal, make them sign them and we witness their signatures and all that – and then we those them away too, leave nothing.'

'Great, just what I was thinking, leave nothing behind. Nothing that they can point to later and say they were manipulated and threatened. It will be as if we were never there at all.'

Miranda choked back a laugh and lifted her glass in a toast. 'Exactly – my idea was to come prepared with lots of convincing papers, and dressed to fit the role, but to leave them wondering if we were a figment of their imagination.' She thought for a moment and added, 'And another thing I thought of was that I want that money transfer to have a comment in one of those fields where you would normally put an invoice number, something to say that Erin is sorry she took the money. So, it looks like she changed her mind.'

Harold gave her a disappointed look and shook his head. 'Really? Do you want Felix to think she regretted what she did and just gave it back?'

Miranda nearly choked on her mouthful of wine, coughed and said decisively, 'God no! No way! That's just for the slight risk that the bank will wonder where all that money in his account suddenly appeared from, you know, if they have some kind of little warning built into their systems. Don't forget it's not the bank he used before, so they have no knowledge of what happened. I thought there was a possibility that any large transaction, particularly from those damned Caymans, might alert some analyst to have a look. And then the analyst would read that detail and maybe not worry.' She took another sip of wine and raised her glass in Harold's direction. 'Anything to avoid that he sees that transaction, or is told about it before I have a chance to do it.'

Fifteen minutes later Harold pulled his glass toward him. 'Cheers! I've never done anything so exciting in my life, I can hardly wait. If you email me exactly what you want on your card tomorrow, I'll get them printed.

And I've got a great idea about mine. Nothing – that's the answer, no detail at all apart from my mobile number and a clever company name. And why will there be no details on my cards? Because the firm I work for flies under the radar and works in such difficult and sensitive areas that we never appear in the media or on the internet – we rely exclusively on word of mouth to get new clients.'

He drank some wine and said in a quite different voice. 'Yes, there is a good reason for that, Sir, we operate under the radar, out of sight. Our clients find us by word of mouth. And yes, madam, we have reported some of our findings to the authorities in the past, but we very rarely have to resort to this. I'm sure you understand why.'

Miranda was deeply impressed. She had never known an actor before, and he was amazingly convincing. Those last few sentences, the change of voice and the way his face became someone else's, someone very serious and scary under that veneer of cold politeness.

'You're incredible! That would convince anyone – I don't know how you do it, just change into someone else like that.'

'I thought about it in the car, what kind of persona this guy needs to have, very formal and polite, and no emotions at all. I want to give the impression of controlled professionalism and a wee bit of threat, but not too obvious, just a hint – did you get it?'

'God yes - it was very impressive! If you turned up and talked to me like that, I would assume you were not to be taken lightly, and more than a bit dangerous. And I'd do whatever you told me to do. Have you got a black suit? And a white shirt and a very conservative tie?'

'I have a white shirt and I'll buy a tie of the right kind, but I only have a grey suit. You want it to be black, do you?'

'I do, I want you to be the man nobody argues with, and I think a man who turns up in a hot holiday place dressed in a black suit and a white shirt kind of fits the image we want you to project. I'll put money into your account for all this, so you go and buy a suit - a lightweight one, remember how hot it will be. And get the cards – oh, and buy a briefcase too, not just any briefcase but a shiny black one and black shoes. We have to look the part, because I think the people that we're dealing with are the kind who judge by appearances.'

'And you, what are you going to look like?'

'Hair pulled back into a low bun, discreet make-up, expensive tailored suit, medium high heels, tiny pearl earrings, no rings – and a briefcase, of course, but not black, something that matches my clothes or my shoes. I'm a woman, after all! And I'm not going to scare anyone, I am just going to be very, very formal and serious and quote a whole lot of legal stuff that I'll look up on the internet.'

They toasted each other and smiled across the table, both exhilarated by the prospect of a shared and slightly risky adventure. When Miranda said this, Harold smiled as if he felt completely relaxed about it. 'But what could go wrong? When they realise we know who they are and that we know everything about them, they can't call the cops, can they? But locating them is another thing altogether, but you said you have some ideas, so I'll leave that to you for now. You do your end, and when we catch up tomorrow, you can tell me what you've found.'

She dropped him at his flat and drove exhausted to her own place, where she booked two return tickets to Spain and sat staring at the screen trying to work out the one thing Harold didn't ask; exactly how she planned to find where Erin and Ralph live. She had no idea where to start and one week to do it.

Chapter 20

Today is Monday, said Miranda to herself when she woke up far too early with her head full of plans and ideas. I must be strategic this week, get my priorities right and not waste any time. I must make a new list. It was so lucky I managed to get next week off now that we're in the final phase of the project, but I did push pretty hard. I must start trying to find out where Erin and Ralph are living, that's the most important thing. If I can't do that, I might as well cancel the whole trip. There's got to be something I haven't thought of, some way of connecting with them. I can't text pretending to be Penny and ask her, that would sound ridiculous. Maybe I can look up some of her friends on her old Facebook page and ask them? But that would be a signal to Erin that something's wrong, if they tell her I've asked – unless I have a totally watertight excuse. And disposable phones, too – I must buy a couple, maybe three, I'll have to work it out. And a suit, something that's serious and classy and elegant, first impressions are important.

She called her office and left a message while the voice message system was still on, to avoid having to answer potential questions. 'Hi, Jodie – it's Miranda, I'm going to be a bit late, please apologize to Richard. I'll be there by ten at the latest. Cheers.'

She was outside the cellphone shop before it opened and waited impatiently while a spotty-faced boy slowly unlocked the sliding glass doors, then followed him into the shop. He disappeared out the back regions to turn on the lights and she found his lack of haste irritating and wondered if anyone had trained him. The fact that a customer was waiting in the shop didn't seem to concern him.

'Can I help you?' he asked when he finally turned up again, and Miranda said without preamble, 'I want three super cheap smart phones please, any make.'

She left ten minutes later with a little carrier bag full of phones and sat on a bench to send an email to Harold from her regular phone.

Hi Harold, I have bought three phones, #1 for me, #2 for you and #3 for my fictitious secretary in London. The numbers are listed below so you can get them on the cards, well #1 and #2 only. I want my card to look like the attached example I found last night on the web, same layout. Just my assumed name 'Carla

*Brooks' at the top, centered, the title, 'Specialist Legal Advisor –
Loss Recovery' below the name, also centered and the #1 phone
number two spaces further down, centered. No company name or
address.*

*I thought it was better that you have a burner phone too, to
avoid potential complications later on. The third number is one
I'll give them if they insist on calling 'my office' to check I'm
genuine. I'll say it's my secretary's number and I'll record a voice
mail greeting trying to sound like someone else. If they want to
check on you, you'll have to improvise. Happy shopping, I'm off
to work now. Talk tonight, Miranda. PS We must discuss
your pay!*

Harold called just after she had finished her
microwaved frozen dinner and they talked for an hour,
mostly about strategies about how to locate Erin and
Ralph, and then he said casually that he had started
writing a script for the confrontation and some
documents.

'A script?' Miranda said, surprised that he used the
word script. 'Do you mean some phrases, or do you
actually mean a detailed script?'

'Lots of detail, lots! Like a film script. We've got to
work on it, so we have a sequence of introductory lines,
that's very important, it sets the scene. I'll introduce us
both, because you are the specialist lawyer – sorry, I
mean legal advisor - that Felix went to and you told

him to contact us as well. So, I'm the heavy, under the polite but menacing title of fraud investigator, and you are the serious, non-smiling legal person. It's important that your lines define you right at the start - not only *what* you say but *how* you say it -it's crucial. It establishes you as a very specific character, that you can then develop further as we talk to them. If you know who you are in that role from the start, you'll be able to ad lib and still stay in character. And we must rehearse it, so you can step into that character and *be* that person.'

'Wow! I can see I got the right guy when I asked you to come in on this. I wouldn't even have known how little I knew. You are now officially promoted to production director and lead actor. I'm going to start working on how to find them tonight, but if you have any new ideas, please tell me so we don't double up on the research.'

Harold said he'd probably be too busy shopping and writing a script to do any research, but he would try to come up with something when he had finished the script. Even before they ended the call, Miranda was pushing her plate to one side and reaching for her laptop. An idea had come to her while they talked, she pulled the pad from last night out of her bag and started searching.

She went back to Erin's Facebook account and tried to remember all those she wrote down as especially close friends of hers, when she did her original research. Now she wrote their names down again, added three she hadn't noticed last time she scrutinized Erin's page and started on stage two. She clicked on the fifteen best friends' cover photos, one by one, and checked each one, looking for those who had no privacy settings. Erin's friends were mostly of the kind who posted endless series of pictures of what they eat and drink, and of their cats, dogs and children. Going through the posts on each of the unsecured pages made Miranda despair of ever finding anything useful. At midnight she ticked off what she had done and retired to bed, exhausted and with tired eyes she couldn't wait to close.

She started again very early the next morning, but by the time she must start getting ready for work, she had found nothing useful. Throughout the day, the thought that she might fail hovered in the back of her mind like a threat, impossible to ignore.

By using her lunch hour to do a fast raid on a couple of shops, she found a lovely, tailored suit in the pale blue of a robin's egg but not the perfect blouse. She returned to the office with the suit in a shiny black carrier bag with fancy plaited cord handles, and Jodie in reception noticed as soon as Miranda walked in. 'Wow – that looks expensive! What have you bought?'

'Just a suit,' she said casually. 'I've got a thing I'm

going to where I have to be formal and I felt a summer dress wouldn't do, so I splashed out.'

In the back of her mind, she tried to conjure up what kind of event this might be where only a suit would do, in June. Her mind refused to cooperate, but the phone rang, Jodie's attention was diverted and Miranda escaped further explanations. In the office she shared with two men, nobody commented on the bag she tucked under her desk. The afternoon flew past and when it was time to leave, she walked out into perfect June weather, still and sunny, and her spirits rose. Tonight, she would continue the search for Erin, she still had four days to find her and there must be a way.

Her flat was a mess with the weekend bag on the floor beside her bed, with only what she had needed last night pulled out, and the things she never tidied up after breakfast were still on the tiny bench and the table. She contemplated the chaos for only a moment, and then the temptation to ignore it won. She pushed a half-drunk cup of cold tea to one side and opened her pad and started the Facebook search again. Halfway through another of those she assumed were Erin's closest friends, she paused to consider if what she was doing really was the best way to find her. Checking hundreds of posts on the pages of Erin's friend who had no security settings in order to find Erin under another name might be a useless pursuit. Maybe Erin didn't only have a new identity on Facebook, but also a new appearance.

And if she had changed herself, would I recognize her? Miranda stared unseeing at the half open wardrobe door and tapped her pen against her front teeth. It's what I would do, if I was on the run. I'd change my hairstyle and dye my hair, maybe I would have a Facebook image of an object, not a picture of myself. A flower or an animal, perhaps. But Erin seemed to be a less careful woman in some respects, despite her talent for planning and deceiving, so heaven knows what she might have done. The only option was probably to continue looking through Facebook posts.

At eight, just when she suddenly realized she was hungry, Felix called. 'How did it go on the drive back - with Harold, I mean?' he said, and she heard the sound of a drawer opening. 'Was it tedious?'

'No, not at all! You can't imagine how wrong we've been about him. He's very interesting! I didn't know until Saturday night that he's an actor, and why Amber hasn't cottoned on to how nice he is, I can't understand. She must have met him lots of times. He's just finished work in a Netflix drama series, and he played out some roles for me, had me totally convinced there was someone else in the car.' A slightly edited story, but she hopes it is justified. If Felix finds out what she is up to, he might ... well, she's not sure what he might do, but he wouldn't approve.

'I know,' said Felix surprisingly. 'I talked to him for quite a while and he's not only very nice, he's also funny in a laid-back deadpan way, very cool, which I always enjoy.'

When they ended the call, Miranda went straight back to her search and managed to work through another couple of Erin's friends before she gave up for the night. Monday night, she thought, only four more evenings to do this. I'm glad I made an excuse for not driving to Exeter on Friday after work, or I would only have one less evening left. And on Monday it's all on and we fly to Spain.

Early in the morning, after a wakeful night when the same questions and thoughts ran through her mind like on an endless loop and prevented proper sleep, Miranda resumed the search. She ate toast with one hand and scrolled down the pages with the other, and then out of nowhere that hashtag, #marblestreet from Erin's text message popped into her mind. She typed it into the search line in Facebook and only three people anywhere in the world had used that precise hashtag. The profile image for the first one was a seaside view, blue water and glistening white buildings; she clicked on it and there it was. She'd found them!

Excitement bubbled through her and she jumped to her feet and danced around her little flat. This might be the luckiest thing ever, she thought, apart from finding Felix, of course, that was the luckiest thing that ever happened to her. She called Harold and when he answered, sounding as if she woke him up, she said, 'Turn your laptop on, I'm sending you an email with a link as we speak, but you need to see the photos on a bigger screen than your phone. I found her!'

Erika L Wilson had only three Facebook friends, and only one was familiar to Miranda, one of the eight she had been investigating most recently. She read the posts over and over while she waited for Harold to get going.

'Are you still holding the phone, or have you gone back to sleep?'

'I'm not holding it, I've got in on speaker, so keep talking,' he said sounding slightly more alert. 'Aha - look at that! There's Ralph the Romeo, sitting on a stone wall with the blue Mediterranean behind him. And still no privacy settings – I can't believe she isn't more careful.'

'I know, she's like a dual personality. And you know how I said I'd keep checking that the house she raved about in those texts is still on the market? Scroll down a bit and you'll see a post about it. She's taken at least a dozen photos of it, and there in the comments is the explanation why the sale hasn't gone through yet, or the purchase, rather.'

One of the comments under a particularly stunning

drone photo of the property was from one of her three friends, whose face Miranda didn't recognize, who wrote, 'I thought you'd have moved in by now!' and Erin/Erika replied, 'Should have, but the owner wanted one more May/June holiday there. It's all on for July, put the champagne in the fridge!'

'*Very* lucky for us,' said Harold and yawned. 'Hey, did you see the one further back, scroll down a bit further - the photo of Ralph on a balcony. Yep! It's him, I recognize him from that race-course photo you showed me and the one where he blocks the view of the fabulous coast. And now he's called Robin! They've kept their initials, that interesting. Probably in case they start saying the wrong name, the old name. So, there he is, leaning on the balcony rail and looking down at his beloved - I bet that's where they live now, a rented flat probably. I'll do some internet snooping while you're at work. Maybe I can work out where this flat is – obviously in Alicante somewhere. I don't even know how big the place is.'

'Did you order the cards?' she asked and started tidying up as she talked. 'And how did you get on buying the suit?'

'You won't believe this, but I found a black suit that fits perfectly and it looks very expensive, but I got it at a forty percent discount, it was in a sale! Saved you heaps of money. It's a manmade fabric, but it doesn't crease and the guy in the shop said it breathes – ludicrous expression, so do I breathe, but I still get hot. I've got the tie and the shoes too, and I'll look for a briefcase tomorrow. I've got an unexpected call to an audition at three this afternoon, which is fantastic – sometimes it's ages between jobs. And I'll pick up the cards tomorrow.'

'Don't forget black socks!' said Miranda and smiled to herself as she did a second trip to the little kitchen-in-a-cupboard. 'I don't think the ones I've seen you in so far are quite right for the part.'

'Right! I hadn't thought of that, all my socks are crazy colours. But we've got a few days yet. Are you going to Exeter for the weekend? And if you are, can I catch a ride?'

She got to work ten minutes early and was alone in the shared office when the CEO walked in.

'I'm very disappointed,' he said, and he sounded as if he meant it. 'I really don't want to lose you! I got your resignation "as of the end of the Grisham Project" – do you mind me asking where you are going? Can I offer you some more money to stay here? Or an office of your own, or an assistant?'

She knew he didn't mean all those things, but it was nice to be appreciated. 'I know where I'm going to live,' she said, 'but I don't have a job to go to. My partner lives in Exeter and I'm moving in with him.'

'Well, I'm not going to change your mind, then. And good luck! Exeter is a lovely city.'

Miranda stood as far away from her nearly full-length mirror as she could in her tiny flat and tried to see herself as someone else might. She was wearing her new suit with a white blouse and she knew she had made a terrible mistake. Even with her hair pulled back she didn't look sharp enough, not serious enough. That's the trouble, she thought, and turned to look at herself from the side. Rushing out in my lunch hour wasn't very clever, I was in too much of a hurry. I really don't want to buy a second suit because I'll never use it. She took the suit off and hung it on a hanger over the edge of the wardrobe door and sat down to read the news online, and then her phone buzzed.

'Hi,' said Harold sounding energetic and cheerful, which only served to emphasize her own low mood. 'I'm sending you some stuff as an email attachment.

Let me know what you think. And how are you, anyway, is everything going OK?'

'I've made a stupid mistake,' she said, and though he might not be interested, he was the only person she could tell. 'I bought a suit and it's the wrong colour, it doesn't make me look serious enough, it's too pale and wimpy. If I wear it with a white blouse, I look like a dressed-up Sunday school teacher and if I wear it with a black blouse, I look like someone's secretary.'

'Go back and change it then. Just pack it up, go back to the shop and say you made a mistake and want to swap it for something else.'

'God, I must be stupid, I never thought of doing that! I kind of think of it as set in concrete when I pay for something. And what is it you're sending?'

'You know how we talked about having some documents for them to sign? We never really discussed what should be in them, but I've done a couple of versions, so let me know what you think.'

The email arrived a few minutes later with two attachments. She read both and sat for a long time thinking before she replied:

Dear Harold, you are without a doubt the most misleading person I ever met. Why is it that I didn't realise from the start that you are practically a genius? Do you stand back in your quiet way at parties and laugh at the rest of us? Talk about clever — these are brilliant. If someone presented me with either of these and said, 'and now you sign here and here' I'd be totally convinced, and I'd carry the threats and consequences in my mind to my dying day. Thank you!

She read the two documents again and then a third time. And then she laughed, and texted Harold: *Please take the extra 'a' out of the phrase "legal recourse"- otherwise perfect! Not that one little typo matters, but it was very reassuring to find that even you can make a little mistake. Thank you!*

The week had disappeared like sand through her fingers and Miranda was excited and terrified in equal parts at the thought of what she was going to do on Monday and also about the weekend ahead in Exeter, where she was going after work today. It was vitally important that she acted as if everything was perfectly normal, that she didn't say or do anything that might alert Felix. There was no doubt in her mind now that he would utterly disapprove of her plan. When she first started planning, she pretended to herself that he might not like it, but that was before she hired Harold, before the reality of fake documents and business cards made it sink in that she was really going to do this, basically perpetrate fraud, however good the intention behind the fraud was. But I have to do it, she told Felix in her mind, it's got to be done, so it's much better you don't know about it until it's done, so you can't stop me.

Overall, the week had gone well. She was able to exchange the suit without any surprised looks and replaced it with an equally expensive one in grey, with little tailoring details in black braid that shout 'money!'

and with the most delicious turquoise silk lining. She and Harold had twice rehearsed the script on Zoom and she was beginning to feel comfortable with her part. Every day she spent some time trying to imagine possible snags in their plans, picturing knocked on that door and what might happen next to prepare herself to react in a way that would fit her assumed persona.

But since last night a nagging feeling of unease had gradually grown stronger. Harold had changed in some marginal way that didn't manifest itself overtly in how he looked or how he talked to her. She studied her reflection in the mirror as she brushed her teeth and tried to work out what it was that she had picked up. Some kind of vibe, like a tiny hint of discomfort or worry when he looked at her, and she was certain that whatever it was he had discovered or thought of had changed their relationship. That Skype chat last night, she thought, and noticed frown lines appear between her eyebrows, what was it that rang false? Like something had changed between our Zoom rehearsal in the morning before I went to work and last night. He might be the world's greatest actor, but I'm nearly certain he's hiding something from me.

She couldn't stop thinking about it and nearly went past her bus stop. She played the conversation back in her mind, tried to identify what had changed; she was sure she was right and he was worried about something, or he was keeping something from her. All through the day the thought nagged at her, and she found it hard to concentrate. She felt that everything now depended on her relationship with Harold. He had become the anchor for the entire enterprise, and she acknowledges to herself that without him the plan might fail.

At six she was waiting outside Harold's flat and tried to decide if she should ask him or wait to see if she could work it out. Maybe it was something else going on in his life, maybe that vibe she picked up related to something personal and had nothing to do with the Spanish venture. She still hadn't made up her mind when he threw his bag on the back seat and got in beside her.

But it only took twenty minutes of sporadic conversation to confirm her fears. Something was troubling him, and though she couldn't put her finger on it she felt it like a change in air pressure. If it was about her or their venture she must find out now. She couldn't continue without knowing what it was, so she pulled into a lay-by, turned the engine off and felt Harold's surprised look.

'Harold,' she said, her voice tense with worry. 'What's the matter? And don't say "nothing" – I know something has changed and it's making me very nervous. Please come out with it!'

He said nothing for so long that she began to feel slightly sick, she couldn't bear to look at his face, just sat with her hands grasping the steering wheel so tightly that her knuckles went white. And then finally, when she was ready to scream at him, he said quietly, 'I found something out that I don't think you know. I didn't want to tell you until this is over, and I'm sorry you've picked it up. I tried to hide it, but I suppose I must tell you now.'

'OK, tell me!'

'When we were trying to locate Erin's new account on Facebook, or anywhere else, you found her under that assumed name. And yesterday I thought she's such a schemer and planner, and so into all the ego stuff, you know, endless selfies etc. So, I wondered if she might have more than one profile. I tried her original surname with her middle name as a first name, and then I tried Erin Huxford, for some reason. I know they weren't married, but she might always have had two, one from before she was with Felix and one after and just called herself Huxford. I've heard of people doing this.'

'And?' Miranda was so nervous now that she sat rigidly upright, unable to turn and look at him.

'There is another Mrs. Huxford.'

She swung around in her seat, confused and upset. 'Well, there's Felix's brother's wife, Amanda, for a start and probably more from different branches of the family and others.'

'No,' said Harold, reluctantly, 'there's a Mrs Huxford in York and she's married to Felix.'

Miranda couldn't breathe properly; her chest would not expand to draw in a breath, she leaned her forehead on the steering wheel and felt Harold's hand on her back. 'Come on, sit back and take a deep breath! Please Miranda, try to be calm!'

He reached over and took hold of her shoulders and forced her back against the seat. 'Breathe – deep and slow. That's right, good girl!'

Slowly she regained control over her mind and body. 'Tell me or show me, please! *Why* has he never told me that he is married? I want to see if it's real, if you're right.'

'I think I'm right,' said Harold with deep regret. He got his phone out and opened the Facebook app, found the right profile and handed her the phone without a word. As she took it out of his hand, she felt his worried eyes on her face, but she couldn't look at him, could not bear for anyone to watch her when she looked at this. She got out of the car and stood with her back against the door, shading the phone with her body and scrolled slowly through the posts.

Chapter 22

Jennifer Huxford posted on Facebook only at long intervals, sometimes not for weeks and had no privacy settings. Her posts were mostly about women friends, her book club, and an amateur theatre group where she helped with the costumes. But twice she posted the same photo, of herself and a much younger Felix standing on a hilltop with an expansive landscape sloping away behind them and backpacks at their feet. The first one Miranda found was posted on the third of February. Jennifer wrote, "I never forget this date, my darling husband. Eighteen years ago, still the love of my life". Miranda stared at the young faces in the photo; there was no doubt whatsoever that it was Felix. She scrolled feverishly further and further back on the page, but there was nothing new, no pictures of Felix, no mention of him, until on the third of February the previous year. The same photo, only this time Jennifer's caption said, 'seventeen years ago'.

Miranda got back into the car, handed the phone to Harold and thought for a moment before she spoke. Her voice sounded as if it belonged to someone who was on the brink of screaming, she could hear it herself, but she couldn't change it.

'I don't think I can cope with this right now. What if I ask him if he's married and he says, he is – why did he never tell me? What else might he not have told me? Everything has happened so fast between us, I never doubted anything about him.'

Harold opened his door wide. 'Let's have some air – this car is getting hotter by the minute. We don't know for sure that they're still married. There's only one other photo of him on that woman's page, apart from the one that she posted twice, the one taken on that hike. Maybe they divorced years ago?'

'But she calls him 'her darling husband'! You might do that if your husband died, I suppose, but not if you're divorced. Not even if you still loved him – if you're divorced then he's no longer your husband. How far back did you look? I never saw another one, just the one from that hilltop twice.'

'You know what Facebook's like, forever changing algorithms and stuffing around with how the system works - they probably just hid or lost a few posts. There was another one between those two anniversary dates. A photo of Felix in Castle Park.'

'Castle Park in Bristol? How long ago?'

'It was posted months ago – let's say January this year, but there was nothing to indicate when the photo was taken. It could be a year old and she posted it later.'

'But what did he look like? Like now, the same age?' Miranda was in the grip of some feverish state of mind where she wanted to put her hands over her ears and hear no more about it, but at the same time she must hear the worst, now, immediately.

'I couldn't tell,' Harold said carefully. 'It was a profile shot, and from a distance, perhaps five or six meters away. He's standing just beside the pineapple fountain. I studied it really closely, and it's definitely him, but I couldn't tell if he looked a lot younger or not, hard to tell from the side.'

'Pineapple fountain, is that the thing that looks like a pinecone?'

'Oh, it's probably not called that, it's just what I always thought it looked like. Yes, that's where it was, you can see the church in the background.'

They were silent for a long time and then Harold said, 'What do you want to do? Can you cope with this weekend without breaking down, or should we turn around and go back?'

'What would we say if we went back? How would we explain it?'

As soon as Harold answered, she realised that he had thought about this while she was outside with his phone; he sounded very definite. 'Let's turn around and go back. I'll text both Tilly and Felix and say we've had to stop in a layby because you're feeling unwell, and I'm driving us back to Bristol. And when we get there, you call Felix and say you have a dose of the real flu, not a cold, you have a fever, and you're going to stay in bed over the weekend.'

'But he'll want to come and look after me, I know he will!' Tears threatened to overflow, and she wiped her eyes with the side of her hand. 'Even if he's still married to that woman, even if he's deceived me, I know he'll want to look after me! He does love me, Harold, he really does!'

'Of course, he loves you! Don't be silly, it's obvious to anyone who sees you together. I'll tell him that he shouldn't come near you, and that I'll see to it that you have supplies of what you need. And then you can call him, or he'll call you, and you can cry and sound sad, because you really are sad and upset. And we go to Spain on Monday, and you talk to him every day and say you are slowly getting better. And of course, he doesn't know you've wrangled next week off work, so it's no different than it would have been before we knew this. You pretend you're back at work, say on

Wednesday or Thursday. Because we aren't stopping this now, are we?'

She only needed to think for a moment, then she wiped her eyes with her fingers again and started the car again. 'No, we're not! That bloody Erin – we can't let her get away with it.'

Harold copied Felix's number from Miranda's phone and sent a text to Tilly and Felix and within minutes first Tilly, then Felix replied. He read the messages out to Miranda, who was driving, despite his offer to do it. Miranda's own phone pinged with message alerts twice, and then a call came through. She stopped abruptly on the side of the road, saw Felix's name and answered.

'Yes, it came over me really suddenly,' she said and reached out to stop Harold from discretely getting out of the car. 'No Harold is driving now - he's just stopped on the side of the road. I think he got a message from Tilly.' And then she started to cry for some reason she didn't understand, and Felix said, 'I'll take the bus up tomorrow, you sound really bad, darling.'

And Miranda pulled herself together and said in a tear-muffled voice, 'No! Absolutely not! You can't, I refuse to let you catch this, it's horrible. And my flat is just a studio with no space for anyone else. Harold said he'll get me medicine or food or anything I need. I'll call you every day, I promise.'

She ended the call and reached for the ignition key,

but Harold stopped her. 'Come on, let me drive. You can't drive if you're going to cry, it's not safe. You can sit in the passenger seat like an invalid and read the message I got from Amber, who was with Tilly when she got my text.'

And that's what they did. Harold drove and Miranda read the text messages and then she opened the web browser on her own phone and searched for "Jennifer Huxford, UK" and after a couple of minutes she found one single mention, apart from the Facebook link. Jennifer came up on a chatroom site about changes to primary education and defined herself as 'primary school teacher, York'. Miranda opened Instagram to check, but if she was there, she wasn't using her name.

Harold parked outside Miranda's flat, handed her car keys over and gave her a hug. 'I'll call you tomorrow,' he said and walked off to catch a bus home. Miranda climbed the stairs very slowly, and her bag felt as if it were full of bricks.

Chapter 23

Early on Monday morning Miranda parked the car in the long-stay parking area at Bristol Airport, and she and Harold walked to the main terminal in a light drizzle.

'Lulsgate Bottom,' he said, as they made their way to their departure lounge. 'Isn't that the best place in the world to build an airport? Bristol could have chosen some place with a normal name, Nailsea for example, but Lulsgate Bottom is so much better. And by the way, did you know that this airport is owned by the Ontario Teachers' Pension Plan?'

'Harold! Have you been Googling things this early in the morning? You'll be drinking wine with breakfast next,' said Miranda, who was slowly getting herself back to sounding normal, though inside her chest was a permanent hard knot of worry and doubt. 'And don't forget, now we must prepare ourselves for people wondering where we are, if we don't respond to messages – or I do, anyway, Felix is bound to keep in touch more than once every day. I'll text him as soon as we're sitting down. I'll tell him that I didn't sleep well and I'm going to turn my phone off and try to have a long sleep.'

'Do you think I'll ever be able to tell Tilly about this?' asked Harold wistfully. 'I know I promised not to tell anyone, but perhaps five years from now?'

'I'm going to leave it to Felix to decide, after I tell him about this venture – and only if it comes off, of course. I 'd love to tell Amber, but then I would have to let her tell Torsten, too. You know how it goes, and the only way to really keep something under wraps is to tell nobody at all. If it's only the three of us, I mean Felix, you and me, then we have total control over it. I've thought about it a lot in the last few days. We three have a vested interest in keeping it quiet, keeping safe from any kind of retribution or public shaming or whatever might happen, we have something to lose. It's not so easy with others. They'll be entertained and surprised, and they might not be able to resist the temptation to share the story. You know, tell just one special friend, who then tells her partner, who tells someone at work. Imagine the tabloids getting hold of this! We'd be on the front page, and it wouldn't stop there. TV people would want to interview us, and they might search out Erin and Ralph and get their side of it. No, I don't think we can tell anyone, ever!'

'I know - you're right, we can't. If this comes off, and if Erin and Ralph discover the deception, are you worried that they might try some kind of retribution?'

'No, I don't think so. Say they tried to harm one of us, or do something to our houses or cars, then we'd report them to the cops as the most likely culprits and tell them the whole story. And we'll produce our evidence of their various crimes, and that would be them taken care of. I'm more concerned about someone hearing about it and taking it on themselves to complain about us doing this by deception. But on the other hand, that probably wouldn't go anywhere anyway, it's not as if we're saying we are something we're not, are we? We aren't going to impersonate real people.'

Harold smiled. 'Of course not, I'm not impersonating anyone – I'm the chief investigator for Fraud Recovery. It's a new business I'm trying to start, and they were our first case, you hired me, that's what I'll say. And then someone will hear about the name and I'll get real clients – and I'll become an internationally sought-after fraud recovery specialist.'

They sat in the departure lounge with take-out coffees, reading news on their phones and occasionally making a comment, until Harold suddenly looked up. 'You know what we were talking about before, about how we have evidence of what those two scumbags did? I know it's all good, solid stuff – the facts about the arson, the money being transferred, well stolen actually and that they must have false passports now, it's all good evidence. But wouldn't it be marvellous if we could video the meeting with them? Imagine if you could show Felix how it played out? You'd keep the video to show your children when they grew up, play it every Christmas or on your wedding anniversary.'

Miranda made no comment on this well-meant fantasy about her future family because she couldn't bear to think of anything further ahead than the coming week, though she knew Harold's reference to her wedding anniversary was an attempt to comfort her. To protect her hard-won composure, she opened her shoulder bag and unzipped the little internal pocket.

'I got this.' She held out a USB stick, thicker and longer than normal. 'It's a recorder, which works on a battery and it can save seventy hours of audio, but you have to charge the battery for every fifteen hours of recording. I bought it a few days ago, and I've tried it – perfect sound. You just plug it into a USB port on your computer or one of those little speakers and play it back.'

She handed it to Harold, and he turned it over in his hands and smiled. 'Very clever! I should have known you'd think of something. I thought of using a phone to video our meeting, and we could have had one of our phones just lying around, not filming anything, just recording sound. But this is far better and you could have it tucked away anywhere. We'll just have to check it records well, if one of us have it in a pocket. I don't imagine it would work if I put it in my new shiny briefcase.'

'Oh no, let's not hide it. My idea was to do record everything openly and say it's standard procedure during all Fraud Recovery investigations. Why not?'

'And if they protest or ask why?'

'We just say it's part of our procedures, we don't explain why. The recording becomes evidence. Say it looks like Ralph is going to punch you in the nose, you ask if he would prefer that we involve the Spanish police, like we discussed during our Plan B talks – and they won't want that. We know they've taken false names, and we know they must have passports in those names to show a Spanish real estate company, and they must have proved to their bank in Spain that they are who they say they are. No way are they going to want to involve the authorities. And I want them to know it's on record, that their recognizable voices are recorded admitting what they did. Call me vengeful if you like, but what that evil woman did to Felix – it nearly broke him, Harold! If you had seen and heard him, that night I first confronted him – it was heartbreaking, and I'll never forget it.'

Then she noticed Harold's expression and realised that he had no idea of how she got to know Felix, he still thought they were already friends before his house burnt down but telling him how it began is the best way to get his buy-in to her plan to keep everything to only the three of them.

'When we have dinner tonight, I'll tell you how it began – I didn't tell you everything when we drove back from Exeter. And do you realise we still haven't decided on your salary? I completely forgot, sorry!'

'For God's sake, Miranda, I don't want any payment – this is the most exciting thing I've ever done! And I've got a new suit and shoes, *and* a briefcase – which I've never had before! Not to mention that I'm about to have four or five days in a lovely place full of Spanish food and wine – that's payment enough.'

To her relief he asked no questions about how she met Felix, and they reverted to reading things on their phone until their flight was called.

'I've never been here before.' Miranda shaded her eyes to look out over the sea from the balcony of her hotel room, where they had met for a planning session. 'I've been to Spain twice but not Alicante. I'm so glad I booked this hotel – it seemed a shame to be here and not have the sea views. I'll call Felix before he calls me, so it's done before we go out and have lunch. The last thing we need now is for him to call when I'm surrounded by people, when I'm supposed to be at home in bed.'

'I took a leaf out of your book and told Tilly a lie, the first one ever. I said I had a tiny role in something being filmed in Bath and might not be available on the phone at various times. She's used to that, I leave the phone in my bag when we're filming, most people do.' He sounded troubled at the thought of lying, and Miranda felt guilty that this enterprise of hers had now involved someone else in difficulties.

'I'm sorry, I never thought of it – that you would have to lie to Tilly. I shouldn't have involved anyone else in this crazy thing.'

'For God's sake, don't start worrying about yet another thing!' said Harold bracingly. 'That's the last damn thing we need, and I can live with a lie here and there if it's for a good reason. And this is for the best reason I can think of, so I'm not going to agonize about it. I was just making a comment.' He turned to face her and gave her a sly smile. 'And I had plenty of practice in lying to my mum. She didn't approve of me roaming around town at night with my mates when I was at high school and I used to say I was at the badminton club, just down the block from our flat. Got away with it too, I wasn't caught out once. In fact, she still doesn't know to this day.'

'A good liar and a great actor from an early age,

such useful talents. Well, thanks for being here, if I haven't said it before. Felix said you were a clever guy when he first met you and he was so right.' And then she thought of something else, a more prosaic topic. 'You know how we talked about appearance before and how awful it would be if they recognise us before or after we confront them. The kind of people we're going to pretend to be, they wouldn't fly out to do a job and then spend days acting like tourists. What if we bump into them somewhere and they recognize us from when we were behaving like holiday makers several days earlier – it just wouldn't fit. I forgot to mention it earlier. I'll show you my camouflage.'

She went back into the room and got the floppy sunhat out of her bag. 'I brought this and I'm going to wear it all the time with my sunglasses. I don't think they'll connect me with the woman in a suit.'

Harold studied her for a moment as if he doubted this statement, then he grinned. 'Just kidding! When you pull it down like that, you're unrecognizable. I can only see your chin and the tip of your nose – or perhaps somebody very short might see a bit more of your face. I brought my baseball cap and sunglasses to wear when we go out, and I bought a fake pair of glasses to wear when I'm the Fraud Recovery man, black frame, very serious looking – found them in a fancy-dress shop for three quid.'

A soon as they left the hotel the bright sunshine and

the warm breeze coming off the Mediterranean lifted Miranda's spirits. The phone call with Felix had made her feel guilty and tense, but now she was suddenly more relaxed than she had been since the aborted journey to Exeter last Friday. It was the change of scene and climate, she thought, like being in a different world where she could momentarily forget or at least suppress her anxiety. Dressed like typical tourists, she and Harold blended in with other holiday makers and the sunlight on her bare arms was like a physical touch of comfort. She pulled her floppy hat down a bit lower and put her sunglasses on.

'Come on, let's find that café the reception guy recommended – the one called Yog something.'

She held out the printed city map the hotel had provided. 'You can be the navigator - but I hope we can walk along that famous marble-paved street at least part of the way, seeing that hashtag turned out to be so important. Fancy only three people in the whole world having used it on Facebook.'

'Yog & Bluffin' had tables set out along the centre of a pedestrian street with big square sun umbrellas mounted directly into the paving.

'This *does* look inviting,' said Harold. 'I hope they don't serve fish and chips or some other typical British thing. I want some genuine Spanish food, something local perhaps. And preferably something I've never had before.'

They ordered lunch, and Harold put the map on the table and pulled his phone out. 'This map might be useful, you know. We know there's a hotel neon sign partially visible from the street where their flat is, we saw it in the balcony photo. But we couldn't see the full name.'

'I did a screenshot of that photo, it's in my photo gallery.' Miranda took her phone out of her bag. 'See, here it is – we can see the Ho for hotel and the C underneath before that building cuts it off. I was going to look it up before we left and ...'

'I looked it up while you were talking to Felix,' said Harold. 'Hotel Castillo, here it is, but it's on a corner so I could only see one neon sign in the photo on the internet – there might be one on the other side too. We'll have to go there and have a good look to see if we can identify which direction the balcony photo was taken from.'

'Delish!' said Miranda when her bacon and sweet corn salad arrived. 'This is great. What's your ... whatever that is?'

'It's a short crusty baguette with something thick and tomato-y draped over it and then chunks of feta and some green leaves and some kind of dark, little berry things. Oh, and some sliced olives.' He takes a big bite and adds, 'Capers, that's what those little berry things are. I've never seen such dark capers before.'

'Probably very old. I bet they go that colour when they're way past their use-by date – they turn black.'

There was only one neon sign on the façade of Hotel Castillo. Miranda turned around and looked out over the city and angled her outstretched arms in a V-shape. 'So, the sign could be seen from anywhere within this triangular section of town and I don't think that Facebook photo was very far away, but it's hard to guess. We'll have to cover quite a bit of ground and constantly look in this direction, whatever the orientation of the street we're in. Let's draw outlines of two or three sectors on the map and cover one at a time street by street, so we can tick them off as we go. I've got a pen in my bag.'

They found a convenient smooth wall and drew outlines of three irregular search areas before setting out, full of optimism. But the heat built up as the afternoon progressed and by half past five, they were more than ready to give up for the day. Leaning against a wall in the shade Miranda took off her hat and fanned her face with it.

'This is so much harder than I thought it would be! God knows we seem to have walked for miles and we've still only covered about half, perhaps only a third. I'm getting a crick in my neck from turning and looking over my shoulder so much.' She wiped her damp forehead with a tissue and felt perspiration break out again, even as she dropped the crumpled tissue into her bag. 'Do you think we can risk giving up for today? I'm dying for a shower and we've got two more days to find them.'

'Let's do another hour and then we'll have finished one whole section.' Harold removed his cap to wipe his forehead with the back of his hand. 'This is the biggest search area and if we complete it, we deserve a drink and dinner.'

Chapter 24

Harold scraped the last of his fabada off his plate, reluctant to miss even one bean. 'I really love the food here, I mean Spanish food,' he says. 'This was just what I needed after that fruitless search. That was so good! And don't think I didn't see that tiny smile – I know I talk about it a lot, but I love food, both eating it and cooking it.'

'Oh, I don't mind you talking about food, it's just that sometimes you seem to start looking forward to the next meal when we've just finished one. It makes me wonder if you have worms. Amber said maybe Tilly fell in love with you because you're such a good cook.'

'I really hope it's something a bit more romantic than that, like my charm or my fabulous body or some other sexy thing.'

'Oh no! Those things are kind of temporary, don't

you think?' asked Miranda, suddenly serious. 'They change as we age, maybe turn into something else, but having a really great talent, like cooking or being good at fixing things in the house, or just being kind – those are things that someone will appreciate forever. I really do think that people pay too much attention to fleeting things, like appearance and bodies, instead of concentrating on qualities that will mean something for years and years.'

'You're completely right,' said Harold. 'I think I've always known this in the back of my mind, that women love a man who can cook. God knows why, when most women can cook too, apart from Tilly of course, who can only just manage a boiled egg. But women seem to like a cooking man – weird, isn't it?'

'It's probably the combination,' says Miranda slowly. 'You know, two very desirable things in one package, nearly contrasting things – the ability to be strong and protective, and the ability to feed and nurture. Irresistible!'

'I can only hope that's how Tilly sees me, but we never know, do we? We think we do, and then we might find out they see us as something totally different.'

'Perhaps it's just me,' says Miranda thoughtfully with a crease between her eyebrows. 'Because both the men I was with before Felix were quite tall and strong, and so is Felix, and he's also kind of solid. And you're tall too – maybe it's skewed my view of men in general.'

'Let's get up really early tomorrow and set out before it's so hot.' Harold studied her face across the table as if he had suddenly realized he didn't know enough about her. 'You don't mind getting up early, do you? I just have this slightly uneasy feeling that if we don't find the place tomorrow, we'll get panicky with only one more day to find them or we might fail.'

'But today wasn't a total failure – we've eliminated more than one third of the part of town we need to search,' said Miranda and leaned sideways to read the blackboard with desserts chalked on it. 'I think we've done quite well. Are you having dessert? Could you lean slightly to your left please? I'm going to try the Spanish flan, whatever it is. And while we wait for dessert, I'll tell you the story I promised you - of how I met Felix.'

'Confronted him, I think was the word you used – or was it not a confrontation?'

'Oh, I *did* confront him, but let me start at the very beginning – picture this ...'

Harold sat spellbound as she described finding the breadcrumbs on the bench at Thornhill and how she searched the house for clues. The waiter arrived to take their dessert order and she continued the story the second he turned around to go back to the kitchen. Somehow giving Harold the full story seemed very important now; she wanted him to understand how amazing the whole thing was. Telling someone else somehow made the parts that only she knew more real even to her, because nobody knew about the inner debate she went through. To make someone else understand how it felt to search the house and how her finds made her certain that whoever was living there, for whatever reason, was a good man. As she continued through the story she felt as if she were living it all over again, it became immediate and fascinating.

Her dessert arrived, she took one mouthful and then another and smiled. 'Gorgeous! It's the best flan I've ever had – and trust me, I've had lots. This one is fluffy and almond-flavoured and the caramelized sugar topping is perfect. I'll have it again tomorrow.' She took another spoonful before she continued. 'So, to get back to finding Felix, which would be a great title for a book, I decided to install CCTV and check him out, figure out what he was doing, like was he there every night, or did he come and go? Before I confronted him, I had to know a bit more about what kind of person he was. I mean, he was super tidy, that was obvious – the breadcrumb incident was a serious slip from his normal standards as far as I could make out.'

When she described installing the camera and sitting in her hotel room watching Felix on that Thursday morning, Harold said, 'Miranda, you are mad! Completely reckless! Do you mean to tell me that watching a total stranger on CCTV for a few minutes made you feel it was safe to go and say hello to him at night on your own? In the dark and up a long driveway from the road, and way out of town?'

She looked at him as if he had totally missed the point. 'But I was sure he was OK by then, ninety-five percent sure at least. Just the way he tidied up after breakfast, so methodical and precise and careful. He pushed his chair in and when he turned and I could see his face full-on one last time before he left – oh, Harold, he looked so sad and lonely, he looked bereft. I could *feel* how lonely he was, how alone! And then he went into the pantry and he didn't come out until after six that evening.'

Harold erupts in a shout of laughter that made half the restaurant clientele turn and stare in their direction. 'He went into the pantry and stayed there all day? You've got to be kidding!'

She explained about the pantry and the ice-cellar and finished her dessert before she picked up the story again. 'And then I went out and bought some wine and a couple of cheeses and crackers, of course, and set out for Thornhill. I parked outside the gates and sat and watched on my phone until I saw he'd finished his dinner and then I went in.'

When she ended the story, Harold said with total conviction, 'Miranda, the day I met you was the best day ever, apart from the day I met Tilly! You look so sane and innocent, but you're actually a total lunatic, a crazy risk-taker, who heads straight into a dangerous situation with no sense of self-preservation at all. I would never have believed it — well, I did begin to wonder about the harmless façade when you told me about your plan, but I had no idea then that you're totally insane.'

'Oh, thank you, Harold,' said Miranda and smiled fondly at him. 'What a lovely compliment!'

Chapter 25

Tuesday morning provided no respite from the heat and relentless sun, and after four hours Miranda was once again leaning exhausted against a wall in the shade.

'This is driving me crazy! We started searching yesterday afternoon and here we are twenty-four hours later, and we still haven't found it. I didn't realise how tricky it would be to walk along and constantly try to look in a certain direction, when the direction changes at every turn. And neither did I realise how many of those damn little shallow balconies there are in this place! We'll just have to start again from the beginning. Why is it that it feels so much hotter here when you're in the direct sun, than it does in England? I mean, provided that the temperature is the same. I'm so hot and thirsty, I feel as if I've been trekking through the Sahara.'

'It's the difference between radiated heat and ambient temperature,' said Harold and rested his shoulders against the wall beside her. 'Here we're closer to the equator than in England, so we're closer to the sun.'

'Really? Or did you just make that up?' Miranda wiped her forehead with the back of her hand and put the hat back on. 'Starting again is such a drag – like we're caught up in a vicious circle that will never end, like Groundhog Day.'

'Yes, but that *did* end, and so will this. It's just that we haven't stopped and looked towards the hotel from exactly the right spot. Let's have a look at the Facebook photo you saved on your phone again.'

They bent over the phone together and suddenly she noticed something. 'Look! See the tiny red thing on the side – I've seen that today! It's the extreme corner of an awning over a window, one of those awnings that have a little edge that hangs down, a scalloped edge. We've walked past it today, I'm sure of it. Do you want to split up? You do one of these search areas and I do the other – and then we text when we find it?'

'No, let's do it together, we don't have two copies of that map with the lines we drew. When we've found it, we'll go back and have a shower and have a final rehearsal over a glass of wine in your room, or mine. If you're right, it won't take that long. We just walk quickly down each street in the two search areas we did today until we spot it. At least red stands out.'

It took another hour and a half to find the right awning. They stood exactly where Erin had when she took the photo and looked up at the balcony and the corner of the hotel nearly hidden behind a building in the middle distance.

'I'll mark it with an x on the map,' said Miranda and turned her back on the balcony. 'Let's walk away in this direction – I know it's not the shortest way back to the hotel, but I'd hate for them to come out on the balcony and see us standing here staring at their flat however well disguised we are.'

'God, I'm so relieved! It feels as if we won the lottery.' Harold sat back in his chair and lifted the glass of wine Miranda had just poured for him. 'And what could be better than a glass of wine after a long cool shower? So now it's nearly time for this production to start. One last rehearsal before we have dinner, and tomorrow we knock on their door and it's all on. And what do we do if they are out? Hang around or go back later?'

'I was thinking about that in the shower, and I think we'd better hire a car. I can't see us going back several times all dressed up in our formal gear, getting hotter and hotter as the day goes on. Erin and Ralph might go for a picnic or a day trip somewhere, be out all day. There's no way I can stay immaculate and cool looking, if I'm sweating like a pig inside my lovely suit. We'll drive to their street and park down the block and walk up, and if they aren't there, we can sit in the car with our water bottles and the air con turned on.'

'Or drive around the block a few times and then try again. Great idea! I hope all the car hire places aren't out at the airport.'

A minute later Miranda looked up from her phone. 'There are several rental car companies within ten minutes' walk from here. I'll book online now. How on earth did people cope before they had smartphones?' And five minutes later she said, 'Right, we've got a VW Polo, automatic, the second cheapest class.'

'I can't wait to see if Erin has changed her appearance   but I expect she looks just the same.'

Miranda gave him a puzzled look. 'Why do you expect that she'll look the same? I thought she'd change her hair colour or something, try to look different.'

He made a kissy face and held his arm up and out at an angle. 'She was a selfie queen on her original Facebook page, wasn't she? Always photos of herself, with or without friends. I think she's quite pleased with the way she looks, so she wouldn't want to change too much or perhaps Ralph doesn't want her to change. And maybe that's why there are no selfies on her new Facebook page – she's switched into her occasional well-planned persona and she's being sensible. Maybe she read something about facial recognition software and how you can search the internet for someone who matches a photo? It's just a hunch I have, she's hard to second-guess, such a random woman. A clever planner and she can play a part to deceive someone for a long time, and then she forgets about privacy settings on her social media page. I'm really looking forward to meeting her.'

While Harold went to his own room to get the printout of the script Miranda thought about what he had said and was certain he was right. The change from every second of her Facebook post being a selfie, to having none at all, it must mean something. She texted Felix and said she was feeling a bit better, but she was tired still and would turn off her phone while she tried to have a sleep.

I've been doing this for several days now, she thought, pretending I'm not well and giving him fake updates, and soon I'll tell him I'm feeling much better. God, how I hope he'll forgive me for all this deception when I finally tell him. And I hope he can explain why he never mentioned he's married, but it's hard to think of a reason that would be good enough. What if we end up never being able to trust each other again?

Thinking of Felix reminded her how lucky it was that Donna had that balance left in her firm's trust account, because it had been just enough to fund this whole project. She wouldn't have been able to set up this expedition without it. Her savings were not nearly enough, and she would have been forced to wait for the next six-monthly interest payment on the government bonds to come through. She was also glad she never told Harold where the money came from, but let him think that she was using her savings to help Felix get his money back, investing in their joint future. She had always been aware that she was regarded as privileged and a bit different by her friends at school, and now they regard her as very lucky to have inherited Thornhill. The last thing she wanted was for people to gossip about the money.

And always in the back of her mind was the thought that it would be good for Felix to feel he had money of his own, to have his assets back. Not that he seems to mind right now, but things could change as time moved on. And why she felt that it would possibly be different for a man than for a woman, who married a wealthy man, she couldn't quite work out.

Perhaps the age-old idea of the man as the provider still colours how we look at things, she thought, even if we're not aware of it, a continuing unconscious bias, maybe going right back to when we were cave dwellers.

'Look how tattered it's getting,' she said and waved her copy of the script in the air when Harold returned. 'I found mine in my bag. We've been through this so many times the paper's wearing out. Don't you think we've done enough rehearsing?'

'No way!' said Harold. 'This has to be perfect, but I'm taking that away.'

He reached over and pulled the script out of her hand. 'You know how I recorded us on my phone when we went through this yesterday? I've just had an idea - this is the final step. I'll play back the dialogue to a certain point and stop it, and one of us should be able to chip in with the next bit, either you or me, doesn't matter, or ad lib something that fits the context. We should be able to practically take over from each other if one of us freezes.'

'God, you're a slave driver! I don't know why Tilly loves you. What a pity I can't warn her.'

They spent an hour taking turns randomly turning the recording off and then Harold called it quits. 'Enough! We are so close to perfect it doesn't matter. But I thought of something yesterday, and it might be a serious snag. If Felix gets that money back, will it mean that he's in possession of money obtained by fraud? No, no – don't look like that! I don't mean the way we're retrieving the money. I mean because it was arson. If Ralph and Erin had been caught, say the fire investigator had figured it out and called in the cops – would the insurance company have paid out? Would this money have gone directly to Felix or would they have withheld it?'

'I thought of that the moment I realised that it *was* arson – because I'm absolutely sure it is.' Miranda got up and opened the balcony door and leaned against the doorframe moving her gaze from Harold to the view and back to Harold. 'So, I investigated on various websites – amazing what you can find out on the internet. If the arson is *not* done by or at the direction of the other party in the relationship, then they would pay out. If there's the slightest indication that the seemingly innocent party is just faking being innocent, and he or she has agreed to share the ill-gotten gains with the arsonist, then they won't pay out, of course. And in this case, with Erin absconding with the money and going to live in another country with another man, *and* under a false name, Felix *would* be entitled to the money, because he clearly had nothing to do with the arson.'

'Always the supreme researcher.' Harold ripped the scripts into tiny bits and threw them in the wastepaper basket under the table. 'Let's go and have dinner – I don't give a toss if it's three hours earlier than the Spaniards like to eat, I'm starving.'

'You're always starving. I don't know how you can be so skinny. I was probably right earlier when I said you might have worms. But come over here first and have a look at this.'Miranda pointed towards the marina. 'See that gigantic motor launch, the one with the dark blue hull, about sixth along at the third jetty - it's got a hot tub on the rear deck.'

She pointed, Harold followed the line of her finger and burst out laughing. 'My God - talk about flagrant! How long have you been watching them?'

'I just noticed a few minutes ago - that's why I got up. Fancy having it off in broad daylight with a huge hotel looking down on you. And look! Now he's ...'

'Turn around!' said Harold. 'I don't think you're old enough to watch this – it just ramped up from X-rated to XX-rated.'

She laughed and mouthed, "no, no, no!" and he shook his head at her.

'Let's turn our phones off, so we don't have to take any tricky calls while we're in a restaurant. I'll call Tilly from my room now and meet you in the foyer.'

Chapter 26

They were sitting in the parked car the next morning, as another heavy shower swept in from the Mediterranean and the windscreen became a blur of running water, and Harold said, 'This was a genius idea. I don't know how we would have coped without a car – we would have had to huddle in some doorway.'

Miranda turned the wipers on for the third time since they parked and left them on in intermittent mode. 'We could have got a car this morning even without booking it, I'm sure - there were dozens of them in that garage. But it is nice to be dry and comfortable, while we wait for them to come back. Maybe we should have brought a pack of cards, we might end up sitting here all day. And I'm very pleased you had an umbrella in your luggage or we might have arrived at their door looking bedraggled and far less impressive.'

She was smiling at the idea that anyone would take an umbrella to Alicante in June, but Harold said seriously, 'I know you think it's funny, but I always take an umbrella. If I went to the Sahara, I'd probably take it.'

'You are unique, my friend and I'll be very happy to share your umbrella.'

'I wonder why they bothered to go out so early when it's raining - you'd think they'd have breakfast in bed and ...' said Harold just as Erin and Ralph appeared at the corner carrying a shopping bag each and trying to share an umbrella. 'Aha – they ran out of supplies! Let's give them not quite enough time to unpack those things, and then we knock on the door. They'll be a bit damp, which is good, caught on the hop and at a disadvantage. She hasn't changed her hair, has she. Still a redhead – an evil, but pretty woman, if you like that kind of voluptuous look. Do you think she's got a bit bustier since those earlier Facebook photos?'

'Definitely,' said Miranda, 'she's packed on quite a bit of weight and so has he. Probably the food.'

They watched the unfortune pair approach their door and then a wind gust tilted the umbrella sideways leaving Erin exposed. Ralph reached for the door handle and tried unsuccessfully to lower the umbrella, keep hold of his bag and open the door at the same time. Erin's stance spoke volumes about her impatience; she pushed him aside and darted through the door to get out of the rain and left him to cope on his own.

'Even better!' exclaimed Miranda, delighted to see such disarray. 'Look at the poor chap – now she's let the door shut and he's still outside and that loaf sticking out of his bag must be getting soggy. We'll give them three minutes to finish arguing about whose fault it is that her hair is a mess and his shopping got wet, and then we go in. Just enough time to park around the corner and walk back.'

They walked quietly up the narrow stairs and stopped on the landing for Miranda to turn on the USB stick recorder. She turned to Harold and pointed at the door, 'Listen!' Inside a woman's high, irritated voice said something they couldn't make out and then a man's rumbling reply.

'Are you ready, Ms. Brooks?' Harold knocked three times, and they heard footsteps approaching. Miranda knew that this moment would sit in her memory for the rest of her life: the slight apprehension, the feeling of anticipation and the surge of excitement. A mix of intense feelings quite unlike anything she had ever experienced before, more electrifying than the night she walked down the hallway to confront Felix in the kitchen at Thornhill. The uncertainty of what kind of man Ralph was, how prone to violence, of how much of a fight Erin would put up, how much impromptu calming down would need to be done before the real performance started, it all contributed to the intensity of the moment.

'Good morning, Miss Lloyd,' said Harold politely when Erin opened the door, and she stood as if frozen for a moment, taken aback by their formal appearance and the briefcases, and not least by the use of her real name. 'Can we come in please? We have some business to discuss.'

Without waiting for Erin to move aside, he advanced two steps and she instinctively moved backwards, away from him. Miranda followed him into a tiny hall and then through an arched doorway into the room with the balcony, a combination kitchen and living room.

Ralph was standing behind the high breakfast bar that divided the room. The shopping was unloaded and strewn over one end of the benchtop and the wet umbrella leaned against the wall in a slowly spreading puddle.

'What the hell? Who are you?' he said, instantly belligerent, when Harold stopped beside the group of seats arranged around a small table in the middle of the room and put his briefcase down.

'Good morning, Mr. Thompson,' he said politely without any sign that he had noticed Ralph's aggressiveness. 'My name is John Smith, senior investigating officer at Fraud Recoveries UK. This is Ms. Brooks, Carla Brooks, an independent legal advisor specializing in loss recovery. May we sit down?'

Without waiting for an answer, he sat down in one of the armchairs, pulled out a handkerchief and slowly wiped a couple of raindrops off his glasses. Miranda sat in the other armchair, her legs neatly parallel and slanted to one side, put her slim, grey suede briefcase on the table and straightened the pencil skirt of her charcoal grey suit. Erin and Ralph stared as if mesmerized, silent and uncertain. The look they exchanged was fear on her side and fury on his. He looked as if he were one second away from becoming physically aggressive.

'We want to discuss the evidence we ...'

'What the fuck are you talking about?' growled Ralph and his hands clenched into fists. 'What bloody evidence? And how dare you come barging in like this – uninvited?'

He was shorter than Harold and muscular but going to fat; the kind of handsome man who can get away with a bit of extra padding until he hits forty-five, and then it takes over and he's suddenly just another overweight middle-aged guy. But right now, he could be dangerous, and Miranda suddenly wondered if Harold knew how to fight, and lightning fast she decided to intervene. Ralph was coming around the end of the breakfast bar and advancing on Harold, his body language was as aggressive as his voice. 'You'd better get out smartly or ...'

'Or what, Mr. Thompson?' interrupted Miranda coolly, trying not to give any indication that she was worried by his bluster, though she was as tense as a spring and found it hard to stay seated and unmoving. She could see the panic behind the bravado and knew he was scared, though being scared might make him more inclined to be violent without considering the consequences. She managed to hold still and looked at him with raised eyebrows. 'Or you will call the police? *Very* unlikely, Mr. Thompson.' Her voice changed to the tone of an order, not loud, just firm and hard, as Harold had taught her. 'Now *sit down*, both of you, and we'll tell you what's going to happen next.'

Erin slumped down on the sofa as if her knees had given way, and after a moments' hesitation Ralph sat down next to her. It's working to plan, thought Miranda excitedly, just what we hoped for – enough seats for four and we've got them sitting side by side, so not much opportunity for silent signals between the two of them, but my God, that was a sticky moment, anything could have happened there. And look at Ralph, I never understood what it means when people say someone is 'glowering', but now I do, he's the perfect illustration.

Harold opened his briefcase. 'Mr. Huxford has engaged Ms. Brooks to act for him in the recovery of the money stolen by Miss Lloyd.'

He put some papers on the little table and continued smoothly. 'And Ms. Brooks engaged me – she has used our company on previous occasions. You are going to sign these documents, two for each of you. They are part of our standard fraud recovery procedure, and Ms. Brooks and I will witness your signatures – your real names, of course, not your Wilson alias. In the first of these documents, you acknowledge that you have no further recourse to any legal measures in this case – in short, you undertake to pay the money back and you will take no further action of any kind, and neither will we. In the second document you attest that all the allegations, the evidence and the conclusions regarding your crimes are correct as stated.'

'Like hell!' exploded Ralph and rose to his feet, but Erin took hold of his hand and restrained him. He didn't sit down, however, but remained standing with fury radiating from him like heat from a furnace. Once again physical action seemed imminent.

Harold didn't get up, though if he had, he would have the advantage of being taller than Ralph. He pointed at the little recording device that Miranda had been holding in her hand since they walked in and just now put on the table. 'I would seriously reconsider any thoughts of violence, Mr. Thompson! This little device is recording everything that is said in this room and simultaneously streaming it to a hard drive in my hotel room. It's standard procedure in these cases. To avoid later claims of intimidation or duress, you understand.'

Miranda glanced at him and marvelled at the way his face, still expressionless, now seemed harder and slightly menacing. Ralph subsided onto the sofa again and Erin clutched his hand in a white-knuckled grip. She had said nothing, not a single word since she opened the door. She knew, thought Miranda, and studied her face. She knew the moment she set eyes on us, perhaps she had been anticipating this, worrying about it and trying to imagine what it would be like, and when she saw us, she gave up on the spot.

'This is the case against you and the evidence we have,' said Miranda calmly. 'I am obliged the read it out to you, so we have it on the recording, so there can be no doubt that you were presented with all the relevant facts.'

She took a document out of her briefcase and resting it on her knees she started speaking without looking at the paper.

'On 29 November last year you, Miss Lloyd, was seen loading boxes into a van outside the garage at 14 Lyme Street, Clifton – the property you shared with

Mr. Huxford, who had left that morning on an overnight visit to a client. This is recorded on a neighbour's CCTV, and you, Mr Thompson, are quite easy to identify as the driver of the van, as is the registration plate.' She made a brief pause for effect. 'On the 30 November a devasting fire broke out at approximately midday and resulted in the total destruction of the Huxford property. The cause of the fire was initially determined to be the faulty wiring of a panel heater in the living room, the insurance company approved the claim, and the money was paid into an account set up for the purpose on the 11 January this year. On 25 January you, Miss Lloyd, moved all but one hundred pounds of the insurance money into an account in another bank and we have copies of all the paperwork from the respective banks - and from there, the next day, you made an international money transfer to a bank account in the Cayman Islands in the name of a shell company, Cormorant Holdings, incorporated in the Cayman Islands three months previously. The Avon Fire and Rescue service are reviewing their findings about the fire due to the additional facts that have come to light, and the conclusion in the incident report is likely to be changed. This will mean that the cause of the fire will most likely be changed from an accidental electrical cause to arson. Aside from you absconding with the insurance money, Miss Lloyd, the fact that you clearly removed some of your possessions the day before the fire raised the level of suspicion.'

She put the paper on the table. 'You may keep this document if you like. And here is my business card with my name and a cell phone number. Feel free to call my secretary any time, the number is a for phone she monitors when I travel.'

'And here is mine.' Harold and puts one of his cards on the table. 'Any questions?'

Erin reached over and picked up Harold's card, which was the closest. 'No address, no phone number? How would we get hold of you then?' It was a desperate and pathetic attack, as if an argument could demolish the case against her. She threw the card back on the table. 'Why don't you just take this to the police?'

'Fraud Recovery UK is a highly specialized company, Miss Lloyd. We have no media or internet presence. International clients find us by word of mouth. Our only aim is to restore what has been stolen to the rightful owner. And may I add that it's very rare that we feel the need to report anyone to the police – for obvious reasons it's not necessary. As I said, our only interest is to recover stolen funds or objects, such as jewellery or paintings for example. When we have accomplished that and the binding contracts are signed, our work is done.'

And then he added, as if he were doing her a

kindness. 'But rest assured, Miss Lloyd, that we will not hesitate to inform the police of your assumed names and last known location, should you ever think of taking any action to the detriment of Mr. Huxford or anyone connected to him. The police can access your current account here via your bank – we have all the details. In the past we have only once needed to inform the police. The outcome was not favourable for the fraudster.' He smiled coldly. 'In fact, I think I can say with total confidence that he's still regretting not complying with us.'

He sat back and looked at Miranda. 'Is there anything you want to add, Ms. Brooks?'

'Yes,' said Miranda and got a second sheet of paper from her briefcase. 'Regarding the property you're contemplating buying here in Alicante – the purchase will of course not go ahead. You will inform the real estate firm today that you have changed your minds. They would not disclose to us if any down-payment had been made or if it would be refundable, but I feel confident that the funds Mr. Thompson brought to this venture will suffice for your needs, should a deposit be non-refundable. The affidavits from witnesses, the information from the three banks and from the Avon Fire service along with the CCTV video of you loading the boxes into the van – those will remain in the safe hands of Fraud Recovery UK along with the recording of this meeting.'

For effect she stopped talking for a long moment and looked without expression at the couple on the sofa before she continued. 'And finally, two things. Spanish police don't look kindly on stolen money invested in property here, which is classed as money laundering, so I would advise against trying to buy anything else. We have a very efficient system for tracking property transactions all over the EU. If you should be so ill-advised as to try, we will inform the Spanish authorities and they will confiscate any further funds you have in this country and any property you have managed to buy.'

Chapter 27

Miranda got up and took the papers Harold had put on the little table. 'Perhaps we can use the kitchen counter for this? It's a more convenient height. I would advise you to read the documents thoroughly before you sign them. It's important that you understand the implications of reneging on the contract. We'll give you copies, so you remember what you have signed, of course.'

She walked around the sofa, pushed the shopping to one side before she put the papers on the counter and turned. 'Miss Lloyd, will you sign first, please?'

Erin got up as if in a daze, she stumbled as she rounded the corner of the sofa and put a hand on the back of it to steady herself. Her hair was ruffled up and drying in a strange set of tufts and her face was pale under her tan. She turned and looked pleadingly at

Ralph, but he wouldn't meet her eyes, his gaze slid sideways to the balcony door; he no longer looked aggressive.

'And now you, Mr. Thompson,' said Miranda when Erin has signed, and her signature had been witnessed. 'Would you please come here.'

Ralph got to his feet and approached with a grim look on his face and for a moment Miranda wondered if he was finally going to snap and punch her, but all he did was sign the papers in silence, without reading them.

'Thank you both!' said Miranda, without displaying any pleasure or emotion, when Ralph's signature had been witnessed. 'Now we come to the crux of this business.'

Harold picked up his briefcase, walked around to the kitchen side of the breakfast bar and got his laptop out. He logged in, looked up the closest Wifi signal and asked politely for the password for their modem. There was no resistance left in either Erin or Ralph and Erin gave him the password.

Harold turned a look at Erin that made her cringe. 'Now, Miss Lloyd, you are going to log in to the Cayman Islands bank, and I'm going to stand right beside you, while you do this. You are then going to let me check the balance in the account before we transfer the money to an account in the United Kingdom. Is this clear?'

My God, thought Miranda, if he looked at me like that, and if I were guilty of anything, or even if I wasn't, I would run for my life – the unspoken menace, unbelievable!

Erin seemed to have the same reaction and asked meekly if she could get her wallet out of her bag. 'I have a note there with the account number and the password,' she explained, and her voice trembled. 'I haven't used it often enough to remember it by heart.'

She was clearly terrified of Harold, and Miranda could understand why. That barely concealed menace and the veneer of chilly courtesy. She herself had felt intimidated just listening and watching.

Erin and Harold remained on the kitchen side of the tall counter and Miranda stood on the living room side keeping an eye on Ralph, who was back on the sofa staring down at his hands that dangled between his knees, the picture of a defeated man.

A few minutes later Harold had logged in to Erin's Cayman Islands bank account and checked the balance. He asked Miranda to read out the SWIFT and IBAN codes and the account number for the transfer, then he swung the laptop around for her to double-check everything before she processed the international transfer. As they had agreed and rehearsed, she put the sheet of paper with the long string of codes and numbers to the left of the laptop and pretended to very slowly check that Harold had entered them correctly, moving her finger along the long row of figures, and then again from the beginning. But her left forefinger was moving along the figures on auto pilot. Her focus was on her right hand which quickly OK'd the transfer of the money into Felix's account and clicked on Pay now. There was a movement behind her, as Ralph walked past her towards the bedroom and slammed the door behind him, and Miranda concentrated on her task.

On the far side of the counter Harold turned to face Erin and spoke very slowly and with an undertone of threat, diverting her attention from Miranda. 'Remember what we have told you, Miss Lloyd. The money due to Mr. Huxford will be returned to him, minus our commission. You have both signed legally binding documents that preclude you from any further interference in Mr. Huxford's life or in the life of anyone connected to him. If any form of revenge is attempted, we will inform the police here and in England. And you will today cancel any arrangements you have made regarding the purchase of the villa. Do you understand?'

Erin nodded. 'Yes, I understand.' Her voice was devoid of resistance, but then she took an unexpected step further. 'Are you going to take Ralph's money too?'

'We have no brief regarding Mr. Thompson. Unless his wife engages us to recover funds on her behalf, we are not interested in his money.'

To Miranda's surprise Erin said, 'Oh, thank you!'

While Harold was carrying out this well-rehearsed smokescreen, Miranda had been busy following her mental checklist. Working fast she had located the account holder's profile menu, clicked on Change Password and entered the new password they had agreed on. Then she went back one step, clicked on Personal Details and changed the contact number to that of her new burner phone and the email address, before she closed the banking app and turned the laptop off.

Harold put the laptop in his briefcase and returned to the living room, Miranda picked up her briefcase and looked around before they made their way out of the door and down the stairs, leaving Erin to realise that the papers and the business cards were no longer on the table.

Chapter 28

As soon as they were inside the car, Miranda drove away, around two further corners and then stopped. She leaned back in her seat and started laughing helplessly and nearly out of control. The mix of excitement and euphoria was nearly overwhelming, and within seconds Harold was laughing too.

'Wow!' she said finally and wiped her eyes. 'That was amazing!'

'Best ever!' agreed Harold. 'I'm starving – must be the excitement.'

The drove back to the hotel in silence, each deep in their own thoughts. When she parked in the hotel car park, Miranda glanced at Harold and smiled at the thought that the excitement of the morning had made him hungry again.

'Let's have lunch as soon as we've changed our

clothes. I booked the car for two days, so we can do an excursion somewhere tomorrow if it the weather improves. I think we deserve a day of leisure.'

'A very classy performance!' said Harold as they walked across the foyer towards the lift. 'I nearly felt sorry for them - those disconsolate faces! Well, maybe not Ralph, his face was just angry and sullen looking, I suppose. You did pick up the USB stick, didn't you?'

'Oh God yes! I wasn't going to let Ralph grab it – I picked it up before I walked over to the breakfast bar, it's in my pocket. I left it on to record every word until we were on the street. That bit you added about the recording being streamed to a computer at the hotel – brilliant improvisation!'

'Inspired by you telling me about the CCTV camera at Thornhill – it must have sat in the back of my mind waiting to be used.'

In the hotel lift, Miranda studied her grey suit and black silk blouse in the full-length mirrors with great satisfaction. 'I'm glad I remembered Gramma's pearls,' she said and adjusted them in the neckline of her black silk blouse. 'They really make this outfit perfect – expensive and conservative, very convincing. And these glasses, aren't they great? I particularly enjoyed looking over them at Erin, I practiced in the mirror.' She looked at her image over the top of the glasses and grinned. 'They're the lowest strength reading glasses you can get from the chemist, but I can see ok – I didn't even realise I still had them on when I drove back. Come and stand beside me and I'll take a photo of us, so we can show Felix.'

She took three pictures, and they stood for a moment in the corridor outside their rooms looking at them on her phone.

'We do look like genuine, serious professionals, don't we?' Harold tilted the phone so he could see better. 'With your hair up, you look so different and both of us with glasses – how could anyone doubt us?'

'I think it's the briefcases,' said Miranda. 'They set the tone. Let's change now and go down to the bar and then we'll have lunch! I can't wait to get out of these clothes.'

Harold arrived in the bar to find Miranda looking like her normal self, entering something on her phone.

'What are you doing? Texting Felix?'

'No, I talked to him while I was changing my clothes. You'll be pleased to hear that I'm feeling a bit better again today and will arrive in Exeter, accompanied by you, on Friday evening, but if feel tired I'll ask you to drive. I shouldn't joke about it and I'll feel a lot better when I have confessed to Felix.' She put the phone down. 'I've ordered champagne, it seems like the appropriate thing to drink today. And I've just entered a few things in my own phone – the new password and the account number from Erin's note. Which incidentally I took while you were giving her that scary pep talk. So now she hasn't got the account number, unless she has it noted somewhere else – and she can't open the account because I changed the password. And if she tries, the bank will alert me on our new email address. I hope we covered all possible angles!'

Miranda was determined to keep their lunch upbeat and celebratory and pushed her worry about Felix's possible wife in York to one side; the worry that had never left her since she found out about Jennifer. It had sat like a silent menace in the back of her mind and she knew that if she started thinking about it, she might lose control and become emotional, and today was a day to celebrate.

'I wonder if the bank will contact you, seeing the password was changed – you know, to check it was you who did it. You did change both the contact number and the email address, didn't you?'

'I forgot to say - sorry! Before I changed my clothes, I turned my laptop on and logged on to that new email address we set up and there was a message from the bank confirming the transfer, with a link to respond. We were right about them having double verification set up - when I clicked on the link, I had to log on again with the new password. So that saved the bacon – if we hadn't thought of changing the email address in the personal details, Erin would have got that message, and she might have been able to stop the transfer.'

'But she couldn't log on, new password,' says Harold. 'But it might have ended up in mess! And you'll be able to check that bank account tomorrow and confirm it's empty. Thank God, we had all those brainstorming sessions about what could possibly go wrong. Proves that saying about two heads, doesn't it? Neither of us would have thought of all the details on our own.'

After lunch Miranda heaved a sigh of relief. 'One and a half days to do nice things. God, I'm so glad this is over. And please don't say you want to have a siesta, let's have an adventure. What should we do? We'll have to save the car excursion until tomorrow because now we've both drunk far too much champagne to drive.'

'I'd like to go up to the top of the mountain in the old part of the city and check out the Castillo – that will be a quiet little adventure,' said Harold. 'I don't think I have the energy for a real one. There's a brochure about the Castille in reception and it sounds great . There's an elevator from downtown that takes you up there for free, open all day until midnight or something.'

'Great idea,' says Miranda. 'It's clearing up nicely now, and a bit of fresh air will do us good after all this food and drink.'

The views from the top of the mountain were

stunning and like the tourists around them, they found it impossible not to take another photo at every second step.

'These views!' Miranda adjusted her sunhat and lowered her phone. 'I must have a hundred pictures already, because I keep seeing some new angle of gorgeousness - I must come back here with Felix.'

And suddenly and without warning anxiety nearly overwhelmed her. She stopped at a low stone wall and looked without focus at the enchanting view of white houses, sandy coves and the blue Mediterranean. Mentioning Felix brought it sharply into her mind again that not only did she need to find out if he was married to Jennifer, but she must also plan ahead and decide what her options are, when he replied. What would she do, if he really was married, if he had lied to her? Should she tell him about the money first or after she has asked about his possible wife?

'I wish I could tell him about the money right away, but I can't do it now,' she said to Harold, who stood quietly watching her agitation. 'And there's no risk he'll notice the money until I get home, he never checks his bank account. Which, of course, contributed to the problem. If he had discovered that Erin's sales commissions no longer went into their joint account, he would have asked questions at the time and got suspicious. I want to see his face when he finds out.' She was silent for a moment and added, 'Both when I tell him to check his account and when I ask him if he's married. It's not the sort of thing you ask over the phone, is it?'

'I hope his bank doesn't notify him.' Harold frowned. 'Not that anyone ever deposited hundreds of thousands into my account, but what if they call their customers when something really momentous happens?'

'There wasn't anything on their webpage about it and I couldn't ask, it would have looked suspicious. But I put that reference in - "your share of ins money as agreed". I had to abbreviate insurance to ins but it's pretty clear. Those detail fields weren't long enough even though I spread it out over the three text boxes. I hope that makes it more normal looking.'

'Well done! God, this is a great view,' said Harold and made no reference to her comment about Felix's wife. 'We could go for a drive tomorrow, just randomly stop here and there, and have lunch in some village. We've done so much intensive planning – let's just be impulsive and just go with the flow, have a real change. Let's go back to the hotel now and have a siesta before we go out for dinner. I'm taking you out tonight – to a very, very good restaurant.'

'Great place to eat, perfect!' Miranda said appreciatively five hours later sitting on Darsena' terrace that jutted out over the water. The evening sky was a dark velvety blue and in the yacht basin the still water reflected elegant white hulls. From a distance she heard music and voices, then someone laughed uproariously, and she smiled.

'I read about Darsena before we left England,' said Harold. 'I'm a bit of a foodie, as you might have noticed, and eating out in really good restaurants is my favourite treat. This place has a five-star rating for its food, but I must admit the setting deserves a few stars too.'

'I don't think you should pay for it, though. I involved you in this crazy scheme and you shouldn't have any expenses because of it and I'm very happy to pay.'

'No way! This is my way of saying thank you – I haven't had so much fun in years, if ever. The only negative is that I can't tell anyone. And congratulations to you, your performance was very classy.'

'Yes, but only thanks to your script and all those rehearsals – I just did what you told me to do.'

'Apart from adding that bit about the CCTV at the neighbour's house, that was a good move and I don't know why we didn't think of that earlier. We're very good at this, improvisations included. Did you notice I inserted an ad hoc thing about us having the details of their bank account, implying we knew they have one in

Spain? It was a bit of a risk, of course, just in case they don't have one, but it passed.'

They smiled at each other, relaxed now and triumphant, and for Miranda there was only one big step remaining.

Chapter 29

Late on Friday afternoon, Harold got out of the car outside Tilly's flat and lifted his bag off the back seat. 'See you soon!' And Miranda turned left at the corner and set out for Thornhill with a feeling of nearly breathless apprehension that intensified the closer she got. The gates were open and by the time she reached the house, Felix had heard the crunch of tyres on the shingle and was standing on the front step.

'How are you?' He enveloped her in a hug as soon as she stepped out of the car. 'Are you really better now?'

She reached up and kissed his chin, smiled and told herself to act normal, not to say anything too soon. 'Of course, I'm better – I'm fine! I've got a very special bottle of champagne to put in the fridge. And then, do you know what I really want to do? I want to go for a walk and see how the flower meadow looks and go into the forest. Don't ask me why, I just thought about it after I dropped Harold off. It's at its best in the forest on an early summer evening with the slanting sunlight, I've always liked it more than in bright daylight.'

Their walk in the wood took them along the path under beaches and oaks, a path that had probably been there for generations. The canopy above their heads was dense and the slanting light from the westering sun created angled bands of light between the tree trunks.

'God, how I love this place!' said Miranda. 'Why didn't you tell me you're married, Felix?'

He stopped abruptly and stared at her in surprise. 'But I'm not married,' he said without looking in the least flustered. 'Where did you get that idea from? I've only been married once, for a very short time and we divorced years ago.'

'You were married to someone called Jennifer? And you're not still married to her?'

'Of course, I'm not still married! I couldn't very well propose to you if I was already married, could I? That marriage was a gigantic mistake on my part – my first mistake with a woman. God, what a record I have now!'

'What happened?'

'We met as students and got married when I finished my degree. She was in love, and I had the totally mistaken idea that getting married to someone who loved you and you liked, but didn't love, was OK. I thought knowing someone really well was a good foundation for a marriage - but of course it wasn't. It was doomed from the start.'

Her feeling of relief was so total that she had to bite the inside of her lip to suppress a sob of relief. 'Why? What happened to change your mind?'

He frowned and shook his head at his own folly. 'It seems a bit mean to tell you about it, but the moment that ring was on Jennifer's finger, she pulled out all the stops. Constant assurances about how much she loved me, wanting to decide how many children we would have, wanting to start a family right away, pressure on me to give consent to any children being brought up in the Catholic faith – and this after having got married in a registry office! It took me no more than a few months to admit to myself that I'd made a gigantic mistake and the only thing I could do was get out quickly before I was bogged down with a house and kids, but I kind of hung on for a while. It seemed so brutal to ask for a divorce straight off. And I know it was my fault. I shouldn't have done it, it was totally stupid - but it's easy to be wise in retrospect. And we did get on extremely well and shared a lot of interests.'

'One last question – did she come to Bristol to see you, quite recently?'

He looked perplexed, started to say something but

changed his mind. 'Yes, she did. She was in Bristol visiting a friend. I don't think she even knew I was living there. She read something about the fire, saw my name and a quote of something I'd said, and somehow, she got hold of my number and texted to ask if we could meet. That was the first time I'd seen her since shortly after the divorce. We met in a park and talked for half an hour, a very sad conversation. She's wasted her life, I think – her religious belief has become a force that rules her life to a point I think is probably unusual these days. Quite obsessive and no exceptions allowed.'

Miranda studied his troubled face and could see he was genuinely sad about Jennifer for some reason. 'How has her religion wasted her life? I don't understand it.'

'When we talked the last time, just after the divorce, she said that she'd never marry again or have children. She said that even though we had a civil wedding, she had gone to confession the day before and made a promise to God in front of a priest that the marriage will be the same as if we had married in church, bind us until death.'

He frowned at the memory and Miranda saw how painful talking about it was for him. 'And then she said the worst thing, that she'd always regard herself as married to me. Like she was putting emotional handcuffs on me. It was a shattering thing to hear, but I didn't really think that it would last, I thought she was bound to marry someone else after a while. She's a nice woman, she wanted to have children – and she would have been a good parent. But obviously I never understood the strength of her religious convictions.'

He looked at Miranda as if he was asking for assurance that she understood how it had made him feel. 'I didn't take it seriously, that statement. You might think I should have, but it was so far outside what I could imagine at the time, at that age. And after the divorce I didn't often think about it, but then when we met in Bristol just after New Year– to find that she had kept that vow, it shook me, it was incomprehensible. But you still haven't told me how you know about Jennifer.'

Miranda knew now that this was where it was going to get tricky. She couldn't tell him that Harold found out, not without explaining why he was searching for possible Mrs Huxfords. So, this was the big moment, confession time, and she must start at the very beginning. There was only one thing she must do first, so she started walking back towards the house. 'I want you to do one thing for me, before I go into the details of how I found out, or rather, who told me. Tell me, have you got a banking app on your phone?'

She knew he probably didn't, but if he did, it would

save her waiting until they were back in the house. He stopped again and looked hard at her, confused and probably worried. 'Banking app? Why?'

'Never mind, just bear with me. This is quite a complex story, so can we please go back to the house right away, so you can log in to your bank? Don't ask me any more questions until you've done that – I won't answer.'

She smiled up at him to soften the demand, which she could see was troubling him, and he was about to say something, but her expression sent a clear message that she wouldn't say anything more just then. They walked back in silence; she reached out and took his hand and curled her fingers firmly around his.

They went straight to the study, where Felix now worked from a new desk more suited to his computer gear, and her grandfather's desk had moved to the side of the room. Felix moved the keyboard for his main computer to one side and opened his laptop, while Miranda stood waiting with her heart beating fast. She held only one thought in her mind, 'Please let it be there!' Ever since she clicked on the Pay Now button on Erin's bank account, she has fretted about the remote possibility that something had gone wrong with the transfer of the money. She had checked twice that it is no longer in the account in the Caymans, but she had no way of checking that it was safely in Felix's account, and the thought that something had gone wrong had eaten away at her composure.

Then Felix turned his head, and his voice was nearly harsh. 'What the hell? Did you put your money into my account? Your money is yours alone, we've agreed on that, and I don't want it.'

'No, no!' She stepped up to the desk and bent over his shoulder to look at the screen where his account balance showed an impressive credit. 'I haven't given you anything - this is from Erin. Look at the reference, read what it says.'

And then she started half laughing and half crying, and she couldn't stop, she laughed until she was breathless. Felix jumped up and took hold of her shoulders to stop her from falling over, then he puts his arms around her and held her tight against his chest until she calmed down.

'What the hell have you done, you crazy girl?' he said with his mouth against her hair. 'How did this happen?'

She stepped away from him and felt as if an oppressive burden had been lifted from her shoulders; her mind was finally able to relax. She took a deep breath to steady herself. 'Let's open that bottle I put in the freezer when I got here, it's a really top-class French champagne, and then we'll go and sit on the terrace, and I will explain everything – absolutely everything, all my secrets.'

While Felix opened the champagne, she got glasses out and put them on a tray with some almonds, and the pate and crackers she bought before they left Bristol. She felt the glances he cast in her direction like little physical touches that bounced lightly off her body. She could imagine how curious he was, how confused and maybe even suspicious, but she refused to meet his eyes and led the way to the terrace.

'Now just one more thing, I'll be back in a second.' She went back inside and returned with her laptop.

'Now!' said Felix and popped the cork. 'Are we finally ready? If you don't tell me within the next few minutes I will expire from curiosity. You didn't threaten her with a gun, did you?'

'A gun - are you mad? Of course not! Where would I get a gun from? I can't believe you think I'd be so insane as to threaten her with a gun!'

'Darling, I believe you could do anything at all, anything – I've never met anyone so resourceful or so fearless, but I must say I think a gun would be going a bit far even for you.'

'Well, that's good! Now you must sit quietly, drink your champagne, and listen to a recording I'm going to play for you on my laptop. It's a recording I made on an audio USB stick this week – Wednesday actually. And don't say *a thing* until it's finished – not a single word! You must hear all of it first, and then I promise I'll explain everything, and you can ask as many questions as you like. But one thing first. My confession – I have lied and lied my way through this, I have lied to practically everyone involved apart from one person, and you must forgive me in advance.'

'You know I'd forgive you anything, I promise. Now, will you please play the damn thing!'

Chapter 30

S he plugged the USB stick into the laptop, cranked up the sound and sat back to enjoy watching his face. The first voice was Miranda's. 'Listen!' and then Harold said, 'Are you ready, Ms. Brooks?'

Felix looked at her as if she was someone he'd never seen before, as he listened to the introductions, the protests and the bluster, the veiled threats, the eventual capitulation, and the instructions about the bank transfer. When they reached the point where Miranda read out the name and number of his bank account his eyes widened, she smiled across the table and held a finger to her lips. The part where Harold gave the menacing pep talk to Erin had him leaning forward, intent on not missing a single word. Then came the sound of footsteps, a door closing and a moment later, the sound of a moped driving past.

'How on earth did you manage all that? And that man's voice - it's Harold, isn't it?'

Knowing how complicated this might become, she thought for a moment. 'Maybe it will be simpler if I tell you chronologically how it developed from the very start, what led to the scene you just heard. And by the way, we've just come back from five days in Alicante, we got back to Bristol just after lunch today, and I didn't have 'flu. And then you can ask questions at the end, because there's a lot of detail that might be missed otherwise.'

She pointed at the USB stick. 'I've actually got the recording saved on my hard drive too, so we could record the explanation as well, right now, straight after what we just listened to. This thing can save untold hours of voice recording and there's a lot of room beforc it's full. Perhaps having the story complete with the lead-up and the planning explained will be a nice thing to have. When we're old we can sit down and listen to it again.'

He sat as if mesmerized and listened to the story: how she decided he might not get the money back for years if he relied on Erin and Ralph buying the house in Alicante and then having it confiscated by the courts after a legal battle. How time, and legal fees, and hassle, would eat up their time and energy and peace of mind.

'It would have been awful,' she said seriously. 'I simply *had* to work out some other way to do it.

Anything was better than the prospect of years of battling through the legal systems in two or even three countries. It would have ruined our lives.'

She picked up the story again, from her first idea of how it could work, to how she involved Harold and how he contributed to the planning, to how they bought the clothes that transformed them into the characters they were playing. She told Felix about the script Harold wrote and how he taught her how to step into a character and be able to improvise credibly, how they rehearsed and rehearsed in the hotel in Alicante.

'Harold was a hard task masker. He had us going through everything, rehearsing and getting used to improvising in character, trying to trip each other up, to flip one of us out of character. But to go back to the practical bits – I told you about the photo on Facebook, the one with Ralph on the balcony. We found their flat because of that hotel sign you see a small part of - kind of to one side and behind a building in the middle distance, a neon hotel sign. I'll show you in a minute. So that's what we did on first day there, on Monday afternoon – we went out armed with that image saved on my phone and a paper map of the city, and we found the hotel, of course, Harold worked out which one it was from the part of the sign we saw in the balcony photo. And then we drew search areas on the map – all the parts where that sign could possibly be seen from. We walked around for hours in the blazing sun, but we didn't find the right balcony. So, on Tuesday we started over and we finally found it. I hired a car and we parked in their street early on Wednesday, but they'd already gone out.'

She told him about Erin and Ralph returning in the rain and the sad comedy of Ralph trying to open the door. 'As soon as they'd gone upstairs, I parked around the nearest corner, so they wouldn't be able to check the car registration when we left – we were obsessive about taking precautions about everything. When we walked in on them, they were at such a disadvantage, taken totally by surprise. Two formally dressed people, very serious and professional, who turn up out of nowhere and know absolutely everything about them, I wish you could have seen it. I nearly felt sorry for them, and they were demolished within minutes.'

Felix shook his head. 'And here I was, thinking you were sick in bed in Bristol and feeling sorry for *you*! I wish I could have seen it, too – the way those two caved in when the legal counsel did her bit. That was brilliantly done, by the way, and that warning talk Harold gave Erin while you were processing the bank transfer, what a great performance.'

'I could never have done this without Harold,' she said seriously, 'never! He gave it the professional polish it needed, and he gave me confidence to act a part, to really be that person. I've got to tell you that Harold is now, after you, my best friend for the rest of my life.'

Felix smiled. 'So long as I come first, of course. But it's going to be difficult to be such good friends with him, if Tilly doesn't know anything about it, isn't it? Won't it look a bit odd to her?'

'We've got that one covered, I think. We refined the details on the way down this afternoon. What has supposedly led to this close and enduring affection between us, is that Harold looked after me when I had the fictional bout of flu. He visited every single day, brought me what I needed and cheered me up, forced me to have a shower, and to eat something, and now we're best friends. He'd already filtered in bits of this, piecemeal, into his conversations with Tilly over the last few days, so she's already used to the idea. And please note that I took a big bottle of sunscreen lotion with me to Spain to avoid coming back with a suspicious looking tan.'

She turned off the recorder when they came to the part of the story she had left to last, the part where she broke down on the way to Exeter, and how they turned around and drove back to Bristol.

'I don't want this on the recording, it's too personal. You have to try to understand,' she said seriously. 'It was a kind of do or die situation. After Harold told me about that other Mrs. Huxford I was in a state of near melt-down. He only told me after I tackled him, asked what was wrong. I could sense it that day, something had changed. Over the days before last Friday, I had talked to him or seen him every day in Bristol while we planned all this, so I knew him really well by then. And on the Friday, suddenly he was troubled by something, and I got so worried that I pulled over on the side of the road and made him tell me what was wrong. If I'd spent the weekend here after hearing that, I could *never* have carried it off without cracking and asked if you were married – and what if you'd said you *were*? Then you'd have asked how I found out, and I couldn't explain it right then, because it would mean I had to confess the whole plan, and how Harold got involved. And if I'd told you the plan, you would have said I couldn't do it, wouldn't you? And the whole thing would have been ruined. Once we were in Spain, it was like being in another universe, and I could concentrate on what I was supposed to be doing and put the worry about you being married to one side, well mostly.'

He said nothing for so long that she wondered how outraged he was about her deception, and then he finally spoke. 'It's impossible to judge what I would have said, now that it's all over - successfully over. I would have either said 'that's totally mad and I don't want you to do it'. Or I might have said, 'I want to come, even if I don't have a part'. And then he smiled and pointed his glass at her. 'Would you have carried on, even if I said not to do it?'

'It's impossible to judge what I would have said or done, now that it's successfully over,' she said coolly, and they both laughed.

Miranda handed her phone over. 'Have a look at the photos. We took them in the lift when we got back to the hotel. We were quite pleased with how we transformed ourselves. I've brought the snazzy briefcase with me today, and those signed documents are still in it and our lovely business cards and my glasses.'

He scrolled through the photos and grinned when he saw Harold in the guise of a Fraud Recovery investigator. 'He looks the part, he really does, and now that I've heard how he talked – that was serious intimidation without him uttering a single threatening word, very scary.'

'The best thing, apart from you getting the money back,' said Miranda, 'is that they can't do anything about it, they can't report us, even if they find out we tricked them. Anything they tell anyone about this will expose them as thieves and we might set in motion a process to get them prosecuted for arson and theft. And all the rest - having false passports, bank accounts in false names and God knows what. They'll simply have to put up with it, and if Ralph's race winnings, or whatever it was, aren't enough to keep them, they'll just have to start working for a living. Erin can't get into the bank account in the Caymans because the logon is changed, as is the email address and the phone number - and there's only a few dollars left there anyway. I didn't tell you that bit – I must check that burner phone now and then to see if anything comes through about someone having tried to access the account. She might do it because she has no idea how much money I transferred back. But I took her note that she had the bank account number on and her logon password, which I then changed. But I think you should move that money from your cheque account to an investment account or something – it's far too much money to have sitting around without earning interest.'

'And you left nothing for them – no papers, or cards?'

'Not a thing! When we packed up our things, Ralph had already retreated to the bedroom, he couldn't bear the sight of us. And Erin was still on the kitchen side of the breakfast bar where Harold was packing up the laptop and putting it in his briefcase, so I just took every single scrap of paper and put it all in my briefcase. There was nothing left to show that we had ever been there – as if we were a figment of their imagination. And before you start feeling sorry for them, remember that they had already transferred quite a bit from Erin's Caymans bank to Spain – I saw it when I was snooping around in the account. We can log in and have a look if you like, so you can see all the transactions before I took the rest. I think they have plenty to go on with.'

Felix leaned over to top up Miranda's glass. 'Let's put this USB stick and the paperwork you got them to sign and your business cards – and of course, the printed-out photos of you and Harold - in a beautiful box and keep it in the study and let it become part of the history of Thornhill.'

They were waiting in the shade of a tree in Cathedral Close. 'The irony of this isn't lost on me,' said Felix. 'In the first wedding I was part of, I married a practicing Catholic in a civil ceremony, and this time I'm marrying an atheist in a cathedral.'

'I know. I hope the cathedral itself won't mind us using it as a setting just because we love it.' Miranda looked down at her new dress and thought what a lovely blue it was and how fitting the colour seemed on this hot July Wednesday, just a shade darker than the sky. 'It's a bit crass, I suppose, to turn it into a commodity, but when I woke up this morning and saw what a perfect day it is, I thought of how the sunlight will make the cathedral windows glow in all their amazing colours. Oh, there's Harold now!'

She waved her arm above her head, and they

watched Harold striding towards them and Miranda smiled at the sight. 'Doesn't he look lovely in his black suit? If he didn't have that grin on his face, you'd be able to imagine him exactly as he was when he was the man from Fraud Recovery – no, he'd have to add the glasses and the briefcase.'

'I'm so hot!' said Harold when he reached them. 'And black is not the colour for a day like this. I thought I should give this suit another outing and wearing it makes me feel very serious, which seems appropriate for the occasion. I've never been a witness at a wedding before. I'll take my jacket and tie off the minute we get out of the cathedral. Where are we going for lunch?'

Felix glanced at Miranda and they shared a smile. 'She said you'd think of lunch long before it's due. We're going to a waterfront restaurant in Torquay. The master planner has gone to great trouble to set everything up, to avoid bumping into anyone who knows us or you. We came in a taxi and a taxi is booked to take us to Torquay and then we'll get another one back to Thornhill. We'll drive you back to Bristol tomorrow – we're going to pack up Miranda's flat. Saves you a trip on the bus.'

Miranda looked at her phone and took Felix's hand. 'Time to go, guys.'

As they walked out of the shade into the bright sunshine, she turned to Harold. 'My flowers are in the cathedral, so I wouldn't stand around looking like a bride – just in case someone saw us and got suspicious. Ever since we decided to get married super privately, I have worried some stray acquaintance would spot us and become a hanger-on.'

Harold looked her up and down. 'I must say you look totally gorgeous, Miranda. That blue really suits you and you don't look like a traditional bride, but the flowers would have been a bit of a give-away, I suppose. Who is the other witness?'

'Mrs. Wylie, my old science teacher – she's waiting in a pew at the front. She's not very well, and she didn't want to stand around in the heat. She's looking after the flowers for me.

Harold laughed. 'Just make sure you marry the right woman if the witness is holding the flowers, Felix. I'd hate all our efforts in Spain to be wasted by this final instalment going wrong. This will be such a lovely surprise at the party on Saturday! Did I tell you I'm picking up my new second-hand car on Friday? When I come down for the weekend I'll be driving.'

'Isn't Torquay pretty?' said Miranda when the waiter had shown them to their table on the terrace of the waterfront restaurant she had chosen. 'We used to come here when I was little, just for a Sunday walk along the Esplanade and afternoon tea and ice cream. What a pity Mrs. Wylie was so tired and decided not to come. She would have enjoyed this – I don't think she gets to go out to a place like this very often.'

'She enjoyed the actual wedding though,' said Felix. 'She told me how flattered she was that we asked her to be a witness. Did you hear what the dean was saying to her when Harold took the photos of us alone afterwards? He said he's never performed a marriage ceremony at nine in the morning on a weekday before – he sounded as if he didn't really approve, but Mrs Wylie just laughed.'

Harold lifted his glass of champagne in a toast. 'Here's to a long and happy marriage!'

'And here's to you, Harold! Thank you!' Miranda took another sip. 'The more I think about what we achieved, the more I realise that without you it wouldn't have worked - or if it had, it wouldn't have been the totally convincing professional performance it was. Your script and all those rehearsals, and your attention to detail, saved the day. I'll be grateful to you forever and so will Felix. I've told him you're my best friend forever now, after him, of course.' She raised her glass in a toast. 'Isn't it great that nobody needs to drive! This is gorgeous and I hope they have a second bottle chilled. I feel like being truly wicked today. And what is this, brunch or lunch? It's like we're having champagne instead of morning tea.'

Felix looked at his watch. 'It's rather early pre-lunch drinks with nibbles, to be followed by lunch. Will you send us the photos, Harold, so we can print them out for the party? Miranda wants a framed photo of us somewhere for people to gradually notice on Saturday. She's bet me ten quid that Amber will notice it before anyone else, wherever we put it.'

'We should put it in the cloakroom off the front hall, she's bound to go there before anyone else – pregnant women are forever needing to pee.'

'I'll email you the photos and then I suppose I'd better delete them from my phone. All these damn things I have to remember to pretend I know nothing about – I wouldn't like Tilly to come across them.'

'I know,' said Miranda and put her hand on his. 'I'm sorry this has involved you in so much deception. But Felix and I have discussed this over the last couple of weeks and we have a plan. We'll have a little party just for us three and Tilly, and Amber and Torsten and tell them the whole story after all. We will sit them down after a lovely dinner and play the recording. You will be interested to hear it again, I think. It is amazing, it sounds like a stage play or a film. And you don't know it yet, but when I played it back for Felix, we recorded my explanations too. How it all started, how you got involved, how we found Erin and went to Spain – the whole thing. If we play them both recordings, we'll all know the same things and there's no need for secrets.'

Felix holds his glass up against the light and studies

the tiny bubbles dancing in the sunlight. 'We discussed it again for the umpteenth time the other day – how long we might need to wait until it's safe to talk openly about it and who we might safely tell. We decided that keeping it to us six, under an oath of secrecy, should be OK. We don't believe there will be any attempt at revenge. Personally, I think they'll avoid ever coming back to southwest England. Ralph doesn't want to bump into his wife or whoever else he deceived, and I'm damn sure Erin won't want to come face-to-face with me. Not after I engaged Carla Brooks and Fraud Recovery's terrifying top man to pursue her.'

Harold nodded. 'I've been thinking about the money angle a lot since we got back. I mean, their money. It's interesting to speculate how much Ralph brought with him. We know what that bloody mansion cost that they were planning to buy, and we know how much Erin had transferred from the Caymans to a Spanish bank, and they'd been living on it for several months already, so the balance in the Caymans account was nowhere near enough to buy the mansion, was it?'

He looked out at the sea and chuckled. 'So, way over there in Alicante or maybe in the Cayman's there must be another account, maybe just in Ralph's name, with a lot of money in it. They're not going to starve, I don't think, but Erin must feel on the back foot with her contribution to their life suddenly gone.'

A waiter refilled their glasses and Miranda waited

for him to leave. 'I bet he won it on the horses or Lotto or Euromillions or something, he's just the type. And I can still hear Erin's voice in my head, after you gave her that intimidating prep talk, Harold – when she asked if you were going to take Ralph's money too, and you said no. She said, "Thank you" in such a pathetic, heartfelt way and she wasn't thinking of just another few thousand going up in smoke, it was a lot more!'

Felix reached for the salmon canapes and passed them to Harold. 'You'd better have some more of these to keep up your strength, lunch is half an hour away. But to go back to how we decided that we should tell Tilly, and Amber and Torsten. We think we should do a whole presentation of it. Show them those documents you put together and the business cards and the photos you took in the lift - we'll swear them to silence before we start and then we'll sit back and watch their faces. Miranda might even tell them how she and I first met.'

Chapter 32

The garden was looking lovely with the late July splendour of roses and herbaceous borders in full bloom. Small tables were set out in the dappled shade at the end of the lawn and to one side was a long table covered in a white cloth, with bins of champagne, and wine and juice on beds of ice.

'What a perfect day for drinks in the garden,' said Amber and hugged Miranda. 'It's not Felix's birthday, is it? Because if it is you should have told us, so we could bring a present.'

'No, no, we just felt like having a party,' said Miranda and caught Harold's eye over Amber's shoulder. 'We thought we should repay some of the hospitality we've had for months now — it's well overdue.'

'Jeez Louise!' Amber turned and saw the full extent

of the preparations. 'My God - this looks like a real production. It's a full-on garden party – is that a real barman or is it a mannequin? How wonderful!'

'We got caterers in to do the lunch, and they provide a barman. Go and get yourselves a drink,' said Felix. 'I can hear more people coming up the drive.'

Torsten, who as usual had stood by listening to Amber with a smile on his face, took her hand and they wandered off towards the bar, followed by Tilly.

Harold lingered for a moment and said quietly, 'I'll bet you ten quid Tilly will notice first, and you should have taken that ring off, Miranda,' before he followed the others across the lawn and another group of guests approach from the drive.

'Put it in your pocket, please,' said Miranda and slipped the ring off her finger. 'Trust Harold to notice – he never misses a detail.'

Felix smiled. 'No wonder he's Fraud Recoveries' top investigator.'

Letters from the Past

Letters from the Past is a series of stand-alone novels where a letter from or about the past reveals something that changes a woman's perceptions of herself or of her family, and that affects her outlook on life.

These books are such fun to write, and I am always working on the next title in this series. I hope you will enjoy reading them as much as I enjoy writing them!

Tina

Having had nobody in her life since her husband died, Lara unexpectedly finds herself involved with three men. One is planning to use her, one she plans to use for her own ends, and one becomes a "friend-with-benefits" with surprising results. Sometimes a quiet schoolteacher is not all she seems at first glance.

Callista experiences an event of apparent ESP at the Okehampton Castle ruins and becomes a media sensation, but the effect it has on her life is dramatic. How do two people, one calm. one seriously claustrophobic, who feel they are poles apart, cope for an hour and a half in total darkness in a stalled lift? And can they handle the consequences?

Sofia's life is in turmoil: a difficult diva mother, a letter with a confession about a family killing and having to accept help from a man she loathes when she is injured. Can reluctant attraction turn into love?

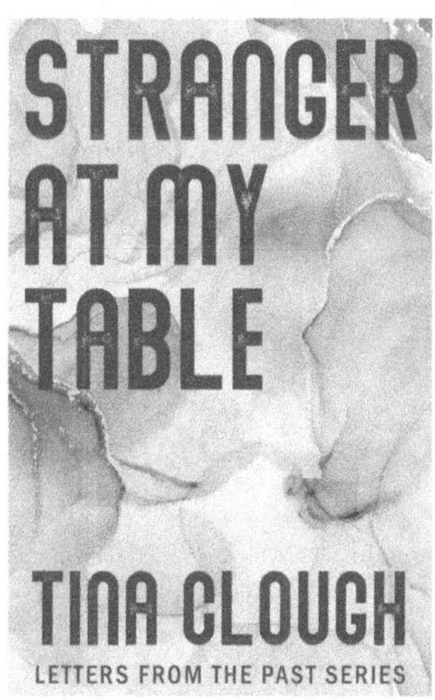

Who is the stranger living in the empty house Miranda inherited from her grandmother? Why is he living like a secretive recluse in someone else's house? Reckless Miranda decides to confront him, and what she discovers prompts her to set out on a fearless quest to bring justice to a man who has given up hope. But is the gamble too great or a risk worth taking?

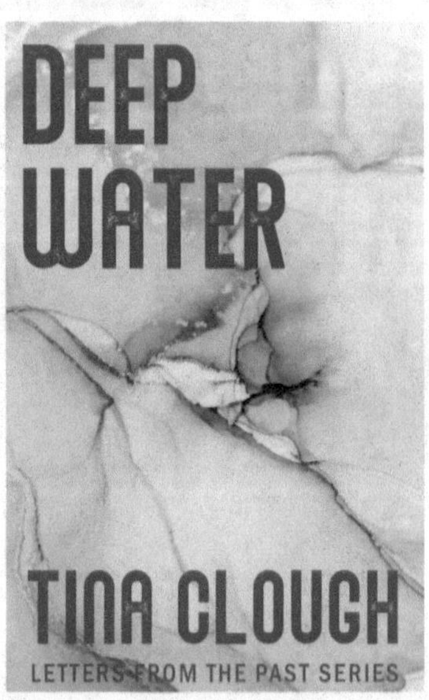

When Emma finds an old letter in a library book she is instantly intrigued, but by researching the origin of the letter she unwittingly opens the door to danger and becomes the target for threats and harassment. Nearly desperate, she takes a leap of blind faith into the unknown and accepts an offer of help from a stranger - but can she trust him?

Jamie, an ardent protester against the gigantic Vista Resort development and Leo Masters, the high-powered developer, seem unlikely to ever agree on anything. But unexpected coincidences and chance brings them together in a fragile state of mutual respect. Will courage and kindness resolve the situation, or do they need help?

After a bizarre accident with ESP overtones, the media haunt Arapera. But can she trust an offer of help from a man she has only met once? Or will she regret it for the rest of her life if she doesn't take the chance? Sometimes life is a knife-edge balance between staying safe and taking risks, and there is no way of predicting if the gamble is worth it.

RUNNING TOWARDS DANGER

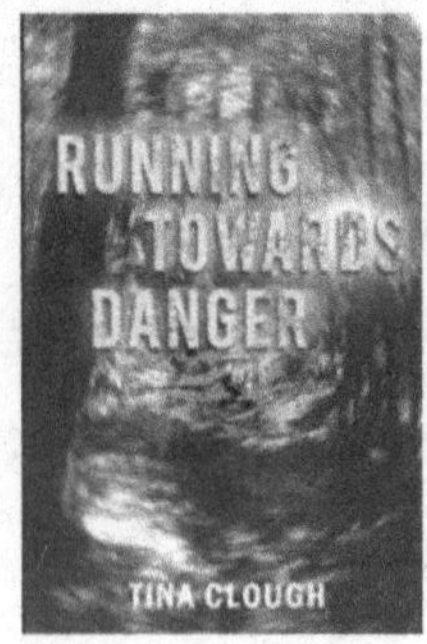

When Karen's flat-mate Nick is gunned down in front of her in the street her life is turned upside-down. Everything she thought she knew about him turns out to be a lie. She becomes a suspect in the police investigation and drug bosses think she knows where Nick has hidden a large sum of money. When her life is threatened, she decides to leave town and disappear.

Karen becomes Cara and creates an anonymous existence, severs all links to her past and adopts a cash-based way of life that leaves no electronic traces. But despite her careful planning danger still stalks her and she is forced to make dramatic choices in the face of threats and brutal violence.

Can she trust the man she is attracted to, or has he been sent by the killers to gain her confidence and find the money they believe she has?

THE CHINESE PROVERB

Book 1 - Hunter Grant Series

Army veteran Hunter Grant thought he had left war behind in Afghanistan – a conflict that left him with physical and psychological scars.

But finding an unconscious girl in the Northland bush and gradually untangling her story involves him in warfare of a different kind in his own country.

Hunter sets out to find and punish the man Dao calls Master, but he soon finds there is more to this story than enslavement. Before long he himself is being hunted by the overlord of a drug empire whose sole objective is to kill Dao because she knows too much.

Protecting her and waging war while trying to keep the police from stifling his enterprise takes all Hunter's ingenuity and determination and puts him in deadly jeopardy.

ONE SINGLE THING

Book 2 - Hunter Grant Series

Journalist Hope Barber disappears two weeks after returning to New Zealand from an assignment in Pakistan, leaving her front door open and her bag and phone inside. The police are tight-lipped about their reluctance to act, and Hunter Grant and Dao agree to help Hope's brother Noah find her. Details about Hope's time in Pakistan gradually emerge but only raise more questions.

Was Hope under surveillance?

Was she linked to terrorists?

And who is the man Hope called 'my stalker'?

FOLDED

Book 3 - Hunter Grant Series

First notes asking for help and folded into tiny origami shapes are found outside a city apartment building, then a physics textbook with tiny writing between the lines and then the woman who found them abruptly resigns and disappears. Are the notes asking for help real or is it a game? Hunter Grant, ex-army and with a pragmatic view of justice, reluctantly agrees to help find the missing woman.

Things get complicated when a high-powered lawyer arrives form the US, and shortly after his meeting with Hunter and Dao, a "cease and desist" letter arrives from the Cayman Islands. Inspector Bakker - a woman, who in Hunter's words "looks as if she would be useful in a brawl, provided she was on your side" - takes instant exception to his involvement and threatens to arrest him for interfering in an investigation.

Dao sets out alone on a dangerous mission, driven by a compulsive need to find out what has happened to the girl who wrote the notes, and Hunter looks death in the face when he decides to risk everything to put an end to the Darknet forces that threaten their lives.

THE SHADOW BROKER

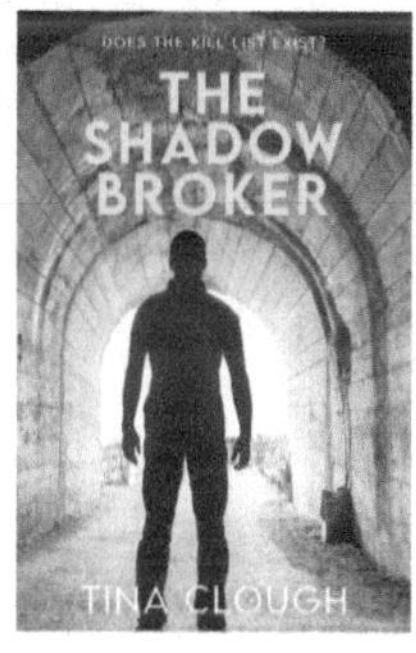

It is 2026 and individual freedoms are severely curtailed, with state surveillance everywhere. State Security has a Watch List, and being on it means that nothing you do or say escapes the authorities, but does the Kill List really exist? And if it does, how would you know if you were on it?

Coded messages on a found burner phone, top-level government corruption and a shadowy mastermind who calls himself The Broker. In this climate of state control, three unlikely friends start quietly looking for connections and set in motion a deadly game of hide and seek that will change their lives forever.

Trying to uncover the truth means risking your life, and nothing is more dangerous than searching for evidence of government corruption.

About the Author

Tina Clough grew up in Sweden and now lives in New Zealand; dividing her time between writing fiction and translating and editing medical research papers.

Between working and writing she looks after an acre of fruit trees, vegetable gardens and roaming hens.

Apart from reading her interests include photography, wine, growing organic vegetables, making jam and kayaking.

https://lightpoolpublishing.com

9 781991 187130